♠ ◇ ♣ ♡ ♠ ◇

DEATH
in the CARDS

by ANN T. SMITH

"THE Stroke of Death. May it forever part our ways."

Clutching this note, Carrie O'Toole Selton, an eccentric and superstitious Boston landlady, was found choked by her own red scarf. Her ancient old house on Brattle Street was sinister enough at best; a corpse did not make it less gloomy. Nor were the assorted tenants whom Mrs. Selton had selected because she had seen them in the "cards" calculated to inspire confidence.

There was, for instance, a rough seaman subject to nightmares and the d.t.'s; and a too suave archeologist with a gruesome collection of skulls.

For once, the Hub's Brahmins spoke to its barbarians, under the impetus of Murder!

♠ ◇ ♣ ♡ ♠ ◇

♠ ◇ ♣ ♡ ♠ ◇ ♣ ♡ ♠ ◇

DEATH
IN THE CARDS

by

ANN T SMITH

PHOENIX PRESS

Publishers :: New York

♠ ◇ ♣ ♡ ♠ ◇ ♣ ♡ ♠ ◇

To

JEANNE AND DOUG

CHAPTER ONE

As I NEARED the old square mansion in Cambridge that early June evening my steps quickened. The day had been hot, unseasonably so, and my nerves were jumping with fatigue. But I felt good. More because of the success of our Radar experiments than because of the coming week's leave. It had been a winter of intensive work for the government—work that I couldn't discuss even with Lita.

Letting the cells of my brain drop away from their usual problems brought me face to face with a new world. The locust trees were in bloom! The hedge had been trimmed. And the roses were as lovely as any we'd had in Oregon.

But the house? That never changed. As square and as uncompromising as the first time we laid eyes on it. Spring or winter made no difference to it. Built a hundred years before of timber, it was still sound as a vault. And that's what Lita sometimes said it was—a burial vault—when I refused to move. But then Lita always over-expressed herself.

She said it that first day—that the house frightened her with its long black shutters. I pointed out the fine old chimneys that topped the trees and the delicate lace wood-work that fringed the roof and the porches. She was stubborn, "A coffin has stiff lace fringe too."

But we were tired that day. We had been apartment hunting—and Boston didn't seem any better hunting ground than more war-industrial-choked cities. We had wandered up the curve of Brattle Street, too discouraged to direct our steps, just looking at the fine old houses.

We were standing outside the hedge. Lita had stopped, her lovely face fatigue-shadowed. I said, "Look at those locust trees. Aren't they magnificent? The seed pods sound like castanets."

"More like death rattles! Let's get back to the hotel, Paul. We won't find anything here. I hate these smug old houses with dozens of rooms, all shut up, while we can't find even a corner!"

A woman's face rose from behind the hedge. At any time it would have been a startling apparition. The eyes were large and brown and liquid. At first glance you thought her young because of her eyes and reddish hair, but the lower part of her face betrayed age. The mouth was wide and sagged at the corners. She had a bright chiffon scarf about her throat. It was orange and her loose smock was a bright green. Her hands clutched withered roses.

Lita had grabbed my arm. Murmuring apologies, I moved back.

She spoke abruptly, "Are you looking for rooms?"

"Yes, we are," I said.

"Come in!"

I was as dumbfounded as Lita, but certainly not as reluctant. She kept protesting as I drew her onto the brick path in the wake of the elderly woman, "Paul! This isn't natural. We don't know . . ."

"Shh! Darling, haven't you ever heard of eccentric New England ladies? She likes us. Who wouldn't? We're nice people."

"But, Paul, this big house . . . All I want is just a room . . . I don't like this!"

I chuckled, "She's probably a witch. Maybe she keeps a dog and she's run out of ration stamps. We may end up going out a chute . . ." Lita gave such a convulsive shudder that I finally had sense enough to realize that she was too tired to listen to my nonsense.

Besides, I had to hurry to reach the front door before it slammed at the woman's back. I pulled Lita gently in with me. We both stopped in the entrance hall. The furnishings were something special. Genuine faded tapestries, Oriental rugs, carved bookcases and tables and chairs. It was dim as a church in the high-ceilinged double drawing-room into which we gaped.

"Well, are you coming?" the woman snapped. She was already beyond the curve of the stairway to the second floor. Lita pulled my hand and we started after her. We looked at each other and smiled. Lita was no longer afraid or tired. That's what the faded luxury did for her. I whispered, "What have we got to lose?"

We followed the length of the hall and went through a doorway after the woman. Dark gleaming wood and fabric faded to a peculiar softness met our gaze. There was an air of rich, heavy brooding as though the rooms had been waiting for us. There were two of them and a bath, plus a cupboard kitchen off the main room. After our brief inspection, Lita sat down in a low needle-point chair, and eased her pumps from her tired feet without exactly taking them off.

The woman said, "Everything must stay just as it is. If you want it, move in."

It wasn't the sort of furniture one got playful with, but there was the question of price. Could we afford this museum outfit? I was amazed to hear Lita say, "We'll take it."

I asked her afterwards how she knew the price would be within our reach. Her logic was simple, "She didn't ask us anything about ourselves—what you did, or where we came from. Therefore she wasn't interested in background or money. She just liked us and wanted to help us out."

We were there two months before we discovered that the turn of the cards had decided our fate. Mrs. Selton, our eccentric landlady, "told" her cards every morning. That morning the Queen of Diamonds and the Jack of Hearts turned up to bring her luck. We were they.

We had a pleasant place to stay, at a price we could afford, because we both fell in the blond category. She had to stretch a point to make my brown, blond. But Lita was the perfect type—a beauteous blonde. So far as I could see, we didn't bring her any luck, but she seemed willing to wait. There were times when I wondered at her patience—the times when Lita kicked up a rumpus. When Lita felt that she had a legitimate grievance she went to bat. She isn't the sort to sulk. But, as I told her, "Old people are queer. You have to make allowances for them. Mrs. Selton's like my Granny: she's sneaky and crafty and stingy, but she's a fine old girl."

There were other people in the large house. Two spinsters of about Mrs. Selton's vintage, very aristocratic and not too eccentric. Miss Brundage was the older. She had soft wrinkles like a newly-dried prune and the voice of a frustrated guinea hen. Miss Lovelace had the finest heritage. She was of the purest blue-blood Beacon Hill stock and claimed that the windows of the house in which her family had lived were the finest purple panes of any in Boston. Lita and I took a sneak trip up there after hearing this. The purple had faded to amethyst and lavender—Lita said Miss Lovelace had probably soaked up some of the purple—which we would have passed off as a proper eccentricity of Boston had we not been initiated into the inner circle.

Brundage was like a sour pudding, heavy and damp, but Lovelace was dainty and quick. We didn't get to know them right away, of course. They ignored us for a solid month, although our rooms adjoined theirs. They had rooms to the front and overlooking the garden where they served high tea every afternoon. They had moved in with Mrs. Selton after her husband's death ten years before.

Dr. Oglesbie was younger than the ladies, perhaps in his late forties. He lived across the hall from them with his grinning skulls arranged around the walls of his room. He was an anthropologist, supposed to be engaged on a book. And he had had some magazine articles printed. Mrs. Selton told us this a few days after we moved in. The good doctor corroborated her statements later, giving us to understand that he was the foremost anthropologist in the country. He was plump and soft and his hands were like those of a fat cherub. I never touched them but I knew they were moist. I didn't like him. And I didn't like the way he looked at Lita—whenever he got a chance. The Misses Lovelace and Brundage did their best to overlook us because we hadn't been born in Boston. I did my best to overlook the dapper doctor because he wasn't my sort—it's all in the view.

Brundage told us once how he happened to be there. She was still shocked after two years. Mrs. Selton had met him in the subway, at Park Street Under. She had a bright scarf on as usual, but the wind from a passing train blew it to one side—exposing the enlargement on her throat. He made an involuntary sound of sympathy at sight of the goiter. This must have impressed her—or maybe it was the cards again. If you follow the cards it isn't difficult to gather a motley group of people to your side. At any rate, she ended up by offering him a room in her large house and gave him most of his meals.

The ladies made such a fuss when they discovered this man in rooms across from theirs that Carrie had to do something about it. She solved the situation by bringing in another male—a young man to tend furnace—evidently believing that there was respectability in numbers.

George was that young man. A tall, taciturn lad from a South Dakota farm, bent on finishing his course at Harvard before the draft caught him.

It took us several weeks, after our arrival, to break through his scowling reserve. Lita and I both knew that he suffered from shyness and too much concentration on his goal, so we persisted until he dropped his guard. As usual, Lita took up the cudgels in his defense and berated Mrs. Selton for not making it easier for the lad. Especially as examinations and the end of the term neared.

It was always, "George, send up more heat," "George, repair the pipe in the bahtroom," "George, trim the hedge," etc., until poor George found little time to bone for his exams. Lita fed him and bolstered his spirit and told Mrs. Selton she was a cruel old woman to devil the boy continually. Mrs. Selton told her to mind her own business,

but of course that was one thing that Lita couldn't do—
she was too kind.

She made George spend most of his time in our rooms
so that he wouldn't be available for the odd jobs. Mrs.
Selton got in the habit of leaving notes under our door
for George. "It's going to be a cold night. Be sure to put
on plenty of coal so the pipes won't freeze."

And once Lita had it hot and heavy with Mrs. Selton.
Lita had begun by appealing to her to ease up on George—
saying that she expected too much for the few dollars a
month she gave him and the room under the attic stairs.
That she should help instead of hindering his graduation.
Mrs. Selton, probably piqued at reference to her stinginess,
replied that he didn't have to be a furnace boy—he should
take up arms for his country—he was acting like a coward
just hiding behind his books. Lita gave some hot reply
and Mrs. Selton accused her of being romantically interested in George. I don't remember what the words were,
as relayed to me by Lita and George, but the gist of
her remarks were that Lita was a hussy and no better than
she should be, and being a dancer and all . . .

For my part, I was glad when Caroline arrived. Not that
I didn't like George. He was intelligent and honest. And
I wasn't the least bit jealous. Lita isn't that sort. But my
own work demanded a tranquil home life, and Caroline
picked up the cudgels in George's behalf, freeing Lita—
or so I thought.

It was only the day after her arrival that George barged

in the front door and faced Mrs. Selton in the drawing-room. He was no longer the servant boy sneaking up the back stairs, hoping to have an hour's uninterrupted bout with his books. Lita and I happened to be coming down the stairs. Lita said, "Why, George is drunk." I nodded. Something must have happened—I had never seen George drunk.

"You old bat! I hope you're satisfied!" He shook his fist under her nose. "I didn't make it! See? I didn't get my degree. Now the Army can have me. And I won't be any good to them. Because I failed! I failed!"

Mrs. Selton glared at him. "Shut up! You've been in a spa. Get up to your room!"

"I'm not going up to my room. I'm going down to enlist. I just wanted you to know it's your fault. Always nagging me and badgering me. Not paying me enough to eat hamburger even . . ."

"You didn't have to stay. You stayed because you're a weakling—a coward—a slacker!"

Caroline had had a taste of her grandmother's tongue. She flew to George's defense. "That's not right—to say those things, Grandmother! He isn't a coward—you can tell by looking at him. And he will fight very nobly for his country."

This was such an unusual speech under the circumstances that I wanted to roar with laughter. Mrs. Selton was unable to answer. She looked from George to Carol and back again, evidently wondering what went on under her nose.

Carol had seemed so soft and young the day before when she arrived so unexpectedly. We heard the commotion of her arrival. It was early in the morning. Although Lita didn't have to be at the New England Conservatory of Music to put her embryonic dancers through their paces for several hours after I left, she usually had coffee with me. Naturally we dropped our cups and raced down the hall to see what the shouting was about. Brundage and Lovelace had their door open but evidently were not yet ready to make an appearance.

This girl with her raven black hair in a silky page boy bob was standing in front of Mrs. Selton. "I'm your granddaughter." There was a soft Southern blur in her voice. Lita pinched my arm—we were under the impression that Mrs. Selton was childless, which was why she had other people live with her.

Lita whispered, "She's darling," and I gave the usual whistle, very pianissimo. She really pinched me then. The girl was a knock-out, sweater girl and pin-up girl in one. She had on a brief cotton dress in jade green. But she might have been the wolf himself about to devour grandmother, judging from that old lady's reactions.

She pushed the lap table and cards to the floor, stumbling over them in getting to her feet. She went close to the girl. "Don't lie to me!"

The girl smiled. "I should have sent a telegram and not surprised you like this . . ." Her voice quavered. "But I didn't have time . . . I didn't have anybody else to turn to . . . Daddy told me that if I ever needed anyone to go right to you."

Mrs. Selton's face hardened. But just then the two old ladies came out of their rooms and my attention was distracted. Brundage was in her usual black with a wisp of lace at the throat. She had on a black hat and white gloves as though she were going to church. Lovelace was in purple silk, cream lace and the inevitable white gloves. She wasn't as much of a hypocrite as Miss Brundage and didn't pretend she was on her way out by wearing a hat. They marched down like a committee from the W.C.T.U. and took up their places behind their old friend, Mrs. Selton.

Mrs. Selton didn't notice them. She was examining the girl feature by feature. "Evie had blond hair. Your hair is black."

The girl smiled sweetly. "Yes, Daddy's hair was black."

Mrs. Selton shuddered. "Where is—where is he?"

We could hardly hear the breathed answer, "He died last month."

Mrs. Selton threw the scarf from her neck and stroked it in a nervous gesture. When she saw the startled look on the girl's face she drew the scarf back and shouted, "Where is Evie?"

"Mother's been dead for two years."

Mrs. Selton tottered back to her chair. She began fanning her face with her scarf. Her voice was harsh when she spoke. "Why did you come here?"

Lita said, "That woman is a devil! Why can't she be human?"

The girl's answer finally came, "I didn't think you would mind. After all, you are my grandmother. I—I was frightened." I thought she was going to break into tears, but she didn't.

"What have you been doing for a month? Where did you come from?"

"I was working in Washington. I wanted to make my own way. I got work as a filing clerk. We lived in Virginia before Daddy died."

"Quit saying 'Daddy'! I don't want to hear about him. I don't suppose he left you anything?"

The girl shook her head. She was biting her lip and tears welled into her eyes. Lita started down but I pulled her back. I was sure that Mrs. Selton would soften up more readily if we stayed out of it, specially Lita.

Miss Brundage spoke up in her sour voice. "Did you come on the train?"

"Yes, I did." The girl had held back her tears. She even smiled.

"Then where are your hat and gloves?"

"I didn't have any. I mean—I have some—in my room. I was at work when I decided to come to grandmother's."

Brundage pursued the subject, "You went to work—like that?"

"Yes," I wondered how the girl could still smile. "Everybody does in Washington. It's right warm there. None of the girls wear hats or gloves."

Had she said they went to work nude, Miss Brundage couldn't have been more shocked. She pronounced her dictum, "The present administration!"

I looked at Mrs. Selton. She seemed to have fallen into a coma. She was staring at this grandchild.

Miss Lovelace took advantage of the silence. "Why did you leave your work so suddenly?"

Color drained from the girl's face. She looked appealingly at her grandmother but got no encouragement. "I was in trouble," she stated simply. "I didn't know how to solve it. I just could never go back to that office." She spoke more rapidly trying to get her explanations over with. "I couldn't go back to my room for my clothes. I had only enough to pay my fare. You don't get your money right quick in the government, you know. You have to wait. I couldn't wait!"

"What kind of trouble?" All three women asked the question but the voice was Mrs. Selton's.

The girl's eyes widened as she looked from one face to the other.

Miss Brundage got impatient. "It was a man!"

"Yes, it was a man!" She spoke defiantly, evidently letting them make the most of it. They did.

Mrs. Selton looked stricken and pitiable. Her friends advised her, "It's not your responsibility, Carrie. There are places for such girls." "How do you know she's your granddaughter? She could have picked up the information."

"She is my granddaughter. This is Evie's sin coming home to roost. Evie said those very words, 'It is a man! And I am going away with him.' I knew when the Queen of Spades turned u pthis morning that something terrible would happen. I thought if I sat still in this chair —but trouble came in to me."

Caroline couldn't wait for any more words—she quietly slumped to the floor. Lita and I were at her side almost before she came to rest. I picked her up in my arms. "Shall I put her in your bed, Mrs. Selton?"

"No! No! You can't do that!" She started wringing her hands. "I don't know what to do. I have no place for her."

"There's the room upstairs," I said quietly. This extra room was between Dr. Oglesbie's and George's. Brundage had said once, "I wish that room weren't there. Carrie is apt to bring 'most anybody in. She is getting more unpredictable by the day."

Mrs. Selton got out of ther chair. She seemed suddenly very old. Her voice had lost some of its brusqueness. "Bring her here." I followed her through the diningroom and into the small kitchen hall. She opened a door that must once have been a butler's pantry. There was a made-up cot against the wall—perhaps for Annie the maid when the weather was too inclement for her to go home. I stood there holding the softly breathing girl and looked around at the clutter of storage boxes. My words were meant to be insulting. "I'll take her up to our rooms. She can have our bed."

"Put her there, damn it!" I was so surprised at this outburst from Mrs. Selton that I obeyed instantly. Lita put a cover over the girl and I asked Mrs. Selton for some whiskey. To my surprise she not only had it, she brought it from the kitchen. The girl had opened her eyes, so I fed her a few spoonsful. At her tremulous smile, Lita said, "We live upstairs, Paul and I. Run up any time—we'd love to have you."

And the next day she was strong enough to stand up to her grandmother for George. That didn't help her case with Mrs. Selton, who was sure now that Carol was man-crazy and must be guarded every minute.

I've never believed in love at first sight because you're apt to believe only your own experiences and Lita and I rather detested each other at first. She thought I was cold and egotistical—one of those guys with a private pipe-line to God—and I thought she was a pretty piece of fluff. The way she would float through the library in one of those interpretive moods of the dance when I was deep in study! I lectured her so much that I almost flunked out. Then I got wise to myself and kissed her. We got married.

With George and Carol it came like a flash. She scolded her grandmother and then she turned to George and smiled—that tremulous smile with the heat turning on slowly until it hit high. George just melted.

He spent even more time in our apartment after that. I discussed the State Department with him. The invasion. I fought the Spanish Civil War over again and made the right moves instead of the wrong ones. Carol would come in. I liked her, too, so I would keep on talking. Until Lita would smile falsely up into my face and say, "You have to wipe the dishes now, Bunny." I hated that word, "Bunny." She always wrinkled her nose at me when she said it and intimated that my brain was padded with fur.

But I caught on after she dragged me into the kitchen cupboard where we could hardly breathe. "For God's sake, can't they smooch without our smothering?"

"No, darling, lovers have to be alone."

"Well, let's go to bed then. At least I can stretch my legs."

She smiled in that "women know best" way. "If her grandmother came up and found us in bed, she wouldn't let Carol come up again."

"Doesn't she know that we go to bed together?"

"Don't try to be funny. Love is a serious business. They haven't much time. George may be in the Army any day and Carol's unhappy."

"How about Carol? Is she in trouble?"

"Paul Redfern, don't be so slimy. Can't you tell Carol is a good girl?"

"No, how can you tell? I always wondered."

"Quit acting like that! She's not in any trouble. She told me about it and I told her just to let the old ladies simmer in their own putrid juices!"

"Phew! It's hot in here."

Lita was whisking the sink clean. "Carol's boss was always making passes at her. She was embarrassed and frightened and she didn't know anybody—you know what a madhouse Washington is—so she just took the first train out. And if that grandmother had an ounce of kindness in her makeup, she'd befriend the poor child." She banged the dishpan under the sink.

"Can we go now?"

"I'll take a peak." She put an eye to the slim opening of the double door. "No, we can't."

She looked so darn cute being grandmother, matchmaker and schoolmarm all at one time that I pulled her over to me. Lita is easy to take. She's sweet and smart and sensible. She looks like a *Harper's Bazaar* model—all smooth lines and eyes that look frankly into yours. We can quarrel like alley cats and then laugh it all off. I kissed her.

CHAPTER TWO

I WAS JUST about to turn up the brick path, still thinking of Lita, when Clancy the cop on the beat hailed me. "How's that bird of ours?" Clancy's a big fellow, all Irish, and with the heart of a child. The week before he had given Lita a fledgling that had met disaster. It was my job to dig worms for it every morning before going to work—and you don't dig worms for a bird without becoming attached to it. Its squawking set the old gals' ears on edge but Lita valiantly defended it.

So it wasn't easy telling Clancy, "It died."

"Now, that's too bad. I always heard they were hard to raise. It's the trees they need and the outdoors."

"It was getting along fine. When we came home the other night there was nothing left of it but a few feathers."

Clancy was shocked. "You don't say! You'd let the cat

in—that big black one they call Beauty?"

"No, we hadn't. Even without the bird Lita wouldn't have Beauty in the apartment—he's too mean. But somebody let him in—and our door was locked too."

"Now, who could have done that—that doctor with the skulls?"

"I don't think so. Beauty wouldn't follow him any place. Lita thinks it was Mrs. Selton."

"Herself?"

"Not purposely, but she has a habit of letting herself into our rooms when the spirit seizes her, and he must have followed. Probably happened before she could stop it. I've seen that beast pounce on birds in the yard. She was pretty sore, though, when Lita accused her of letting Beauty in. Never saw her so angry. I don't know why she didn't bounce us out on our ear. Lita wanted to move but I calmed her down."

Clancy was very fond of Lita. "And why don't you move? That old house is no place for a young girl."

"Well, don't tell her so, Clancy. Where can you get anything now? Besides, I like to walk and it's close enough to M.I.T."

"Well, I best be getting on," Clancy said. "Nothing ever happens, but I got to keep moving. I might stir up a breeze, anyway."

"It is hot, isn't it? Drop up for a glass of ale if you can make it. Have to celebrate tonight—have a whole week to loaf."

He gave me the wink and went on down the tree-shaded street. He was everything a cop should be—tough outside and soft inside. He liked a cold glass of ale—called it the poor man's whiskey and often dropped up the back way to have a glass with us.

The house was quiet as I entered. Mrs. Selton was sitting in her usual high-backed chair. I couldn't see her face but a brilliant scarf end hung over the chair back. Subdued sounds from the kitchen meant that Carol was busy. That was another grudge that Lita had against Mrs. Selton. She had dismissed the maid and saw to it that Carol did all of the work. And the poor kid didn't know a skillet from a broom handle. In Virginia they'd always had a colored maid, as she expressed it.

But it wasn't my worry. I took the steps three at a time, strode the length of the hall and opened the door. "Hello, Queenie!" a playful allusion to her being Queen of Hearts.

"Hello, Jack!" She came out of the tiny kitchen, or rather, turned around. "Feeling pretty fit tonight, aren't you?" Our kiss was long and satisfactory.

"Yes, but don't get ideas. I don't want to go any place. Where are my slippers? I just want to stretch my legs and drink ale and listen to the radio. And I don't want the place all cluttered up with love's young dream."

"Don't be stodgy. You'd think you were a thousand years old instead of only a few years older than George. If they want to come in tonight, they're welcome. You're settling down too fast."

"My shape is still good, so I presume you refer to my great mental powers. Well, let me tell you I could never act as love-sick as George if I was ten years younger than he. I just happen to be a serious guy."

She came over and sat in my lap before I could get my second shoe off and started rumpling my hair. It was going to be a swell week. "Dinner ready?"

"So? You'd rather eat than kiss me?"

"I can do both—now let's eat."

Lita jumped up in mock anger and I put on my slippers. "Let's have a bottle of ale." I got a bottle out. That was one of our surprises—a genuine electric refrigerator in that ancient house. We thought we were in velvet to have the old brocades and antique furniture and hadn't even noticed the modern bath fixtures at first. It's just as well we didn't. Sometimes they reminded me of fakes on a movie set. You never could tell when they would calmly regurgitate all that you had been unwise enough to burden them with. But the refrigerator worked like a dream.

"Hey! Where's the bottle opener?"

Lita flew to the catch-all drawer in the highboy. We usually tossed everything in there, which simplified our housekeeping. Lita was sputtering indignantly, "That old lady's been in here again! That old—"

"Watch your words, my girl."

"Well, she makes me furious. I don't see why she can't mind her own business."

"Don't tell me she's borrowed the bottle opener?"

"No—" Lita handed the innocent gadget to me—"but she's taken the back scratcher. I saw it here this morning right on top. I remember thinking about it several times today. It looked so much like a hand."

"What did you expect it to look like—a foot?" I opened the bottle of ale. "If the old girl can find some use for it—more power to her. I hope she keeps it. Never did like it. And I wondered at the time why the good doctor gave it to you. He could have given you one of his skulls."

Lita's lovely eyes were clouded as she sat down to drink her ale. She was apt to let small things upset her, but only for a moment. Her eyes twinkled just as quickly as they had clouded. "You were jealous of the doctor."

"Sure I was. The way he looks at you would make any husband jealous. I always want to bop him on the schnozzle."

"He's just interested in people's heads."

"So? For your information he doesn't stare at your head when you dance. That makes me think. This is Saturday night. If they pull one of those soirees on us tonight, I'll barricade the door. God knows that's one thing I couldn't stomach tonight."

"Why, Paul, think of the pleasure we give those old people. I've got a lot of practice out of it. I think it's been fun. In fact, it's the only thing I have liked about the house. There's something touching about their performances."

"Yes—Lovelace touching the harp. You'd think she was

on a podium tossing notes to swine."

"Did you ever notice her hands—they're beautiful."

"She's never done anything but play the harp with them."

"And Brundage reciting!" Lita giggled.

"If anything ever happens to her I'll know it's Paul Revere. The way she drags that poor guy out of the grave and sends him galloping through the drawing-room—a vicious form of sacrilege."

"Maybe Dr. Oglesbie will give us the 'Cremation of Sam McGee' again."

"Fat chance! The old girls nearly choked."

Lita set the small table by the window that faced on the lawn and our small Victory Garden. Mrs. Selton had permitted us to disturb the aged peonies and other perennials to do our bit for victory. But she resolutely refused to let us touch the roses. "Tomorrow I'll do some weeding, when and if the old gals go off to church. George certainly hasn't done his share lately."

"How do you expect him to think of tomatoes and carrots now? He's in love."

"So am I—but I do my share."

Lita threw a dishwiper at me. "If you don't quit being so smug, I'll make you wash the dishes. You haven't even asked me how my recital came out."

"Well, how did it? How did the fat little one do?"

"Which one?" More giggling than the remark warranted. But it was a fact—Lita had as fine an assortment of heavily built young females as I'd even seen. I prompted her, "You know, the one who looks like a matador."

"Oh, Francesca! She really did very well. Her parents thought so, and Papa Mateoti kissed me smack on the lips and Mama shook all over with pleasure. Come wipe the dishes, lazybones."

As I leaned over to snub out my cigarette, I saw a white slip of paper being shoved under the door. I walked over and picked it up. "Hurrah! We're in luck!" I mimicked Mrs. Selton's speech as I read, " 'There will be no soiree tonight.' Thank God for that. And it doesn't look as though Carol and George were coming in. This is going to be a very fine evening, Mrs. Redfern."

Lita looked around and smiled at me. "Here, put my ring in the drawer, and then come and wipe the dishes before I have to yell again."

"Okay. Okay. Keep your blood pressure down. I had hoped you would remember that this was my vacation." I dropped the ring on top of the paper in my hand and put it in a corner of the drawer—I'd paid—well, several dollars for that diamond.

I had picked up the first dish when we heard a high scream from the lower floor. The dish fell back in the drainer. Lita dropped a cup on the floor and didn't notice. Her voice was full of fear. "That's Carol!" We raced up the hall to the stairs.

The two old ladies were ahead of us, below the curve of the stairs, too concentrated to notice us. Miss Brundage looked about to fall over the balustrade, her wrinkled face working. Miss Lovelace looked shocked. It was evidently Mrs. Selton who had screamed, and she was still doing a pretty good job. "I won't have you traipsing around getting into more trouble!"

Carol's face was white as she stared back at her grandmother. "If I'm in trouble already, why should you mind my going out with George? You don't want me to have any pleasure."

"Pleasure! You talk like a street walker! You're worse even than your mother."

I thought for a moment that Carol was going to strike her grandmother. She made a move toward her, her hands clenched. Then color flooded her face and her lips trembled. "I'm going to a movie with George." It was a statement, simple and definite.

A tch-ing sound from Brundage drew my attention to her face. Suddenly I was ashamed that we were sharing her avidity. "Come on," I said to Lita, "let's go back."

She pulled away from me, her urge to help Carol dominant. "No! This is a good time for a show-down. That old lady is vicious!"

I hung on to Lita. We weren't going to get mixed up in this family row, no matter where our sympathies lay. George was coming down the hall. One look at his face and I wanted to hang on to him. He must have heard Mrs. Selton's screech about the street walker. His features were twisted in that bitter, stubborn look that we had come to know.

I was glad that Mrs. Selton had changed to a wheedling tone. "Stay with me tonight, Caroline. I'll fix things so you will be sure to get everything I have . . ."

Carol was shocked. "I don't want your money. You just want to keep me in . . ."

It was unfortunate that Mrs. Selton looked up and saw George coming down the steps. She must have seen that she couldn't keep those two apart. She screamed at Carol, "You're just like your mother! You'll play the same trick on me! She left with a man! Ran away in the night! And she wasn't married! You're—you're a—"

"Don't say it!" George was a terrifying object as he advanced on her. Lita sputtered, "That old woman ought to be choked." Lovelace turned on her. "She's right! You ought to be ashamed!"

Mrs. Selton hadn't been intimidated by George. She shrieked as the two of them went out the door, "Nobody will want to marry you now!"

The door closed after them and Mrs. Selton walked slowly toward her bedroom, just off the long drawing-room. I could see the books of the former library still lining the walls. It seemed that somebody ought to comfort the old lady. She would not put up such a fight for Carol if she didn't love her. It was her way of showing it that was wrong. How would they ever heal the breach now?

"Come on, Lita." I hurried her back to our rooms and closed the door. It was all too much for me, and besides, it wasn't any of our business. "That's the last time we're going to be spectators at anything that happens in this house. It's not part of our rental obligations. I feel like an underhanded, sneaking gossip-monger."

"Well, I don't! All those old people stick together, and if we don't back up Carol and George, they never will find happiness."

I took her in my arms. "Darling, can't you understand that people have to work out things for themselves? You saw George tonight—ready to do battle for Carol. And Carol was no shrinking violet. I'll bet on her and on George."

She protested even under the warmth of my kiss. "Don't be stupid, Paul. Old people always have the advantage—if only because they don't want anything. They've lived their lives and all they want is to keep young people from getting anything."

I laughed and kissed her harder. "You're going to mind your own business, Mrs. Redfern, if I have to divert your attention every minute. This is our vacation—yours and mine—and I'm going to enjoy mine!"

She relaxed. There was still the glint of armored righteousness in her lovely eyes, but her lips smiled and her arms pulled me closer. After a few minutes I turned on the radio. Lita ran to the window. "Paul! They're still standing on the corner. Oh, Paul, they don't know what to do!"

I swooped her up in my arms and dropped her on the

love seat. "All they have to do is walk away from the corner." I lighted a cigarette and put it between her inviting lips. "I see that I'm going to have to beat you to get your undivided attention tonight."

That was evidently amusing enough to bring laughter to her eyes. She was teasing me now. "It's starting to rain."

"Good. Relieve some of this heat." A crash of thunder broke the rhythm of the dance tune on the radio and sent Lita unreservedly into my arms. It was a honey of a storm —buckets of rain, stabs of lightning and ear-splitting claps of thunder. And the soft strains of love songs underneath it all.

Finally Lita whispered, "We must close the windows, Paul. The draperies." I obliged by moving the draperies out of the way. The Pops Concert was coming on. I turned it up and moved my chair so I could look at Lita. For the millionth time I thought how really beautiful she was. Not in the usual pretty-blonde way. Her features are strong, more like those of a Greek goddess. And her hair isn't curly. It has only a slight wave, but it frames her face in the most natural way. She's all-of-a-piece, a finished product. She would look just the same if you met her on a mountain top or even in the middle of the desert. I got up and got some ale.

I saw her eyes close. My own felt drowsy. She opened her eyes and smiled at me. She raised her voice above the symphony of violins. "Just like we were in the balcony."

I shouted back, raising my glass to her, "Better. Here we can drink and not have to stare thirstily down on the main-floorers." When we sat in the balcony at Symphony Hall the sound struck us full in the face and we loved it.

Lita was asleep. I put down my glass and closed my eyes. The good music and the thunder in the distance, fainter now . . .

Something was standing in front of me. It was black and immobile. My eyes opened again and I stumbled to my feet. "Miss Brundage! I thought I was seeing things."

"I couldn't make you hear with that radio blaring."

I turned the radio down and called Lita. She straightened up. "Oh, Miss Brundage! Sit down." I drew a chair forward for the sour one, already beginning one of her querulous monologues. "It's been terrible—all the excitement in the house. Evelyn has one of her migraine attacks. You don't know how your radio annoys her! She asked me to have you turn it down. All that noise! And things used to be so peaceful in this house."

"I can imagine." I reached over and shut the radio off. If we had to be miserable we might as well be real miserable. The old lady had her hands folded in her lap and was staring at the empty ale bottles and the glasses. The wind had risen—our door opened silently. Staccato voices came up from the lower floor.

Lita spoke in that quick way she has. "Who's down there? Is that George?"

Miss Brundage sighed. "I'm sure I don't know. Evelyn

wanted me to go down to borrow some aspirin, but I thought I would wait in here until the quarreling stopped. Carrie was saying, 'Get out and stay out! Don't ever come in this house again!'"

Lita got up. "Surely she won't drive them out in this storm?"

"For God's sake, Lita!" I exploded. "It's not snowing. Don't be melodramatic."

She walked over to the windows. "Well, it's raining cats and dogs. They didn't have an umbrella—that's probably why they came back." She walked swiftly into the bathroom and came out with the bottle of aspirin. "Here, Miss Brundage. You won't have to go downstairs now. Take these to Miss Lovelace and I hope her headache gets better."

Brundage took the bottle but she didn't move. She jumped when the door slammed and quiet returned to the lower floor, but she appeared lost in thought. We waited. I had one of those queer feelings that time was being stretched to the breaking point. Perhaps it was the moisture in the air that had eased the fibers of the old house. All through the winter it had snapped and creaked until you were sure that stealthy steps were coming closer in the dark. Lita would stir in her sleep and snuggle nearer. I told her that I liked a haunted house.

Tonight there was no sound but the soft, far-off plop of a roof drain on sod. The house was waiting . . .

Miss Brundage broke the silence, almost a whisper,

looking down at her small brown hands. "Evelyn must have fallen off to sleep." Her drooping face lighted with a tinge of humor. "She is apt to do that once I am out of the apartment."

Lita said, "I'm afraid you've spoiled her—sounds perverse to me."

"I dare say. Yes, I have always spoiled her. It was easier, and then she was so talented and so lovely. We were at Wellesley . . . my parents tried so hard, but I never shone in anything. Evelyn was so popular . . . when she noticed me I couldn't believe it. Her being kind to me was my only compensation . . . even now." Our pity was engaged by her confession. We had always made so much fun of her sour nature.

To cover our confusion Lita and I began to talk at the same time. We talked of the garden. Lita said she would do all of the tomato canning and even make catsup. We let Miss Brundage tell us stories of the old house. It had belonged to the Walsh family. "In this very room Nina Walsh tried to stab herself." Our eyes followed Miss Brundage's to the faded carpet as though we could still see the blood spots. I looked over at Lita—her eyes were large with fright. "I knew something had happened here. I could feel it. She died, didn't she?"

"No, she lived to be eighty, but she lost her mind."

I laughed for no good reason, but I couldn't break the mood. Lita exclaimed, "That was horrible! Did you know her?"

Brundage smiled. "No. My grandmother used to talk about it. Nobody knew her. She was a foreigner, and Jeremy Walsh got what he deserved for jilting a New England girl." She got up, the subject no longer interesting to her in spite of Lita's questions.

I went to the door with her. She said, "If Evelyn isn't asleep—she sleeps in the sitting room—I'll give her the aspirin and then may I come back? When she suffers so I can't sleep either."

"By all means. We can play whist or even charades." I left the door open and turned back into the room. "I guess I'm just a sucker for girls of whatever age."

"I'm glad you are, darling." I got a luscious kiss as reward. Then, "What did I tell you about this house? I knew something terrible had happened here. Imagine that poor woman going mad through all those years here."

"Lita! Use your head. People don't go mad unless they have a predilection for madness, and then it doesn't matter where they live." I walked over to the radio thinking I could turn it on very low. "We've probably missed all the concert."

It was just signing off. Lita looked out in the hall, then closed our door. "Her Ladyship must have gone to sleep, migraine or no migraine. I suppose poor Brundage sneaked off to bed." ·

I snapped the radio off. "How about our doing likewise?"

"Don't be Brooklynese, darling." She was digging around

in the highboy drawer.

"Now what?" In a truculent husband voice.

"I'm going down to pay the rent."

"For God's sake, Lita, not tonight. The old girl's probably tucked in."

She was counting some bills. "She's bound to wake up in the night and remember. You know how she insists on getting it Saturday night."

I kept watching her, some stubborn streak in me wanting to dominate. It was true—we always paid our rent on Saturday. Mrs. Selton acted as though our small rental stood between her and starvation. But I was tired. And I'd had enough of the whole household for one night. "Why is it so important if we miss once? She's argued with everybody else tonight—she'll probably argue with you if you go down."

"Well, if she says anything to me, I'll be glad to tell her a few things. Besides, Paul, if she's driven George out and Carol's alone, crying, I'll just talk to her a minute."

I was a heel, but I was too tired to care. "Okay. I'm going to bed. Probably be asleep when you get back." I slumped in a chair and lighted a cigarette. But I was too restless to sit still. I got up again and took the ale bottles to the sink and rinsed them. Ditto with the glasses. My thoughts kept churning around. Why the devil couldn't we keep out of the problems of the people in the house?

Then I heard it—a pitiful moaning like a small animal in pain. I dashed out the door. Lita was standing at the head of the stairs, as though she couldn't take another step. She said, "Paul," very softly. As dim as the hall was, her appearance startled me—she looked like a sleepwalker.

I had her in my arms with no recollection of having taken the steps to reach her. "What's the matter? Are you hurt?" I was carrying her to our rooms. She was shaking her head and moaning. Once inside, she articulated, "Lock it, Paul. Lock the door."

I did and placed her on the sofa. She didn't seem to be injured. "Whatever happened to you, honey? Did Mrs. Selton say something to you? I'll go down and call the doctor—you look white as a sheet."

"No, no, Paul!" She rallied. "I'm all right, really I am." Her eyes, strangely dull, left the door and focused on me. She tried to smile but made only a small grimace. "I'll get you a drink of whiskey," I said.

After she had swallowed the diluted whiskey, a faint flush crept into her cheeks. I spoke calmly. "Tell me now, what happened?"

"It wasn't anything, really. I—I got frightened . . ."

"You didn't talk to Mrs. Selton? You didn't pay the rent?"

Her hand, still clutching the bills, raised up. The fingers opened and the bills fell to the floor and Lita gave a deep sigh. I said, "After that talk of Brundage's you thought you saw a ghost? That was it, wasn't it? That place is spooky as the devil down there at night."

Surprisingly she started to cry—and Lita never cries.

"It's a terrible place. Let's move, Paul. Let's move right away." She raised up. "Let's move tonight!"

I knew then that something was wrong. She hadn't been merely frightened—she was in a panic. Lita is not the evasive sort—if she has a fault it is in being too forthright, too anxious to speak her mind. "I'm going downstairs." My voice was firm. What in God's name was down there? "You will be all right here until I get back."

She pulled at my shirt. "No, Paul! Please! Don't go downstairs." She became hysterical. "Whatever you do, don't go down there. Don't tell anybody I was down there. Just stay here with me . . . until they come!"

"Until who comes?" I shook her. "Lita, for God's sake, tell me! Is somebody dead?"

She nodded. "Yes. That's it—she's dead. We can't do anything. It's horrible, Paul." She had covered her eyes and was weeping uncontrollably again.

I straightened myself and tucked my shirt in. "It's Mrs. Selton. She had a stroke? I better go down, honey, and call the doctor. He might be able to do something."

"He can't do anything!" She was losing patience with me. "Don't be a fool, Paul! Can't you see we'll be blamed?"

"You mean it's murder?"

"Yes."

She was watching my face. I didn't feel heroic. But I knew what I had to do. "The police have to be notified in that case. I'll be back as soon as I can." I went out and closed the door, the sound of Lita's weeping in my ears.

The hall was miles long, eerie in its dim blue light that only accentuated the bulky shadows that seemed to waver as I approached them. I had never known the house to be so quiet, as though it were gathering force for a demoniac scream. My feet found the stairs. I stopped on the last one. She must be in her chair—a blood red scarf hung over the back. Then I saw something move by the arm rest—my heart floated up for air. She wasn't dead after all. Poor Lita must have been mistaken.

"Mrs. Selton!" My voice sounded strange to my ears. There was only the rose-shaded light that made a small pool by the curtained windows. But it was sufficient!

I stood in front of her chair. Something moved, but it wasn't Mrs. Selton. I had to hold myself rigid to keep from falling forward. The creature that could still move was the Smoke Persian, "Beauty," his eyes glowing hatefully.

Mrs. Selton was dead. There was no doubt of that. Her face, purple from congealed blood, was like a hideous mask, with the tongue—The eyes fascinated me, luminous and child-like . . . reaching out into space.

I backed away out into the hall, the trailing ends of the chiffon scarf that was so tightly tied about her neck holding my attention. I picked up the telephone and dialed Operator. "The Police Station." My tongue was so thick that I had to repeat it, "The Police Station."

CHAPTER THREE

MY RESPONSES must have made sense but they were automatic. There was the number of the house, Mrs. Selton's name and my own. To escape the sight of the blood-red scarf ends, my eyes focused on the design of the Oriental carpet. Something glinted on a scrap of crushed paper just beneath the chair. "Yes, I'll be here. Of course. No, nothing will be disturbed."

I knew as I spoke what the glittering object was. And the knowledge was like an electric shock on taut nerves. The thing that lay, that glinted just beneath the chair of death was one of Lita's earrings.

The phone dropped out of my hands. I took the few steps and bent over. But even before my fingers closed clumsily on the scrap of paper, I knew that somebody was in the room—was behind me, maybe at that moment bending over me . . .

The cords in my neck stiffened. I jumped backward, straightening myself, my hand stuffing the paper into my trouser pocket.

He stood there—seedy-looking, his small eyes regarding me suspiciously. His long arms hung limply. He raised a rough hand and brushed it across his mouth. I saw then, when he swayed, that he was very drunk. He looked like a seaman—I had seen many like him in Scollay Square, even to the cap.

"What do you want here?"

He raised his hand stiffly, warning me to lower my voice. He couldn't control his own voice which grated harshly. "I want to go to bed. She told me I could. Paid the old lady other day."

He could have stepped from behind the drapery. I hadn't heard the door open. He looked brutal, capable of murder. The door was probably unlocked. The drunk-act might be a blind. Those big hands could have knotted the bit of silk at Mrs. Selton's throat as easily as I knotted my shoe lace. And he didn't look as though it would mean any more to him.

He knew the old lady was sitting in the chair but he made no move toward her—he seemed to know that she was dead. He kept edging away from her—toward the stair. Lita was up there—our door open. The thought that he was probably here when she was down—that Lita might have been killed by this—

I shouted at him, "Stay when you are!"

He looked ugly as his head turned in my direction. His arm swung up. It looked like a hammer. I knew he could make hash of me in spite of my height, but I moved in, like a fool. The hammer dropped—to his side. "Listen, Mac, I don't want no trouble. I'm tired. Where's that room?"

Until the police came, the room was a good idea—if he meant it. I went up the steps ahead of him and waited. Then I walked to the spare room, opened it and showed him the bed. He flopped over on it. The key was in the lock. I slipped it out and locked him in.

It wasn't real—none of it. Lita sobbing—waiting for me. Brundage and Lovelace in their rooms, not sticking their heads out. Dr. Oglesbie silent in his. And Mrs. Selton growing cold in her chair, her face distorted in death. Beauty squirmed on her lap, trying to find the old comfort, the warmth.

The storm had beat itself out. Why didn't the police come? The back door opened. I heard it, and the heavy steps going up. I bounded up the stairs just in time to see a bulky form back out of our room. I was still going when he turned. "Thank God, it's you, Clancy!"

We had almost collided. His face was grim as he pinioned my arms. "You gave me a turn! This hall is as dark as a dungeon." He released me and took my arm in a friendly grasp. "Your wife told me. I can't be believing it yet. Who could have done such a thing to a kind old lady—God rest her soul!"

We were walking down the hall. "I don't know. I feel too numb to think." I stopped in front of the spare room. "There's a man in there. Here's the key. He was in the hall right after I found the body. Said Mrs. Selton had rented him a room—it seemed a good idea to lock him up until the police come."

Clancy looked his surprise. "That's queer now. If he murdered her why would he want to stick around?"

"It's too much for me. For one thing he's drunk to the point of forgetfulness, and for another he may just be acting smart."

We had reached the bottom of the steps. I noticed that Clancy was as reluctant as I to go any farther. His big shoes seemed weighted as he stepped in front of the chair. "Holy Mother of God!" I heard him say reverently. He made the Sign of the Cross. Beauty stirred restlessly as he always did if a stranger approached him.

Clancy whispered as he rejoined me, "That beast on her lap! It don't seem right and her dead!"

"She was devoted to him. It seemed the only creature left that she could lavish love on." I put my hand to my throat, "Somebody twisted her scarf tight."

Clancy exclaimed, "God save the mark! Don't ever point to yourself—you might be next."

I didn't laugh. My hand fell from my neck. Clancy was serious and so was I. He looked at the telephone. "Did you report it? Did you call our number, Trowbridge

9800?"

"I gave it to the operator."

"I better call again." He went over and dialed the number. "Mary, this is Clancy. Did the call come in—murder on Brattle? Were you able to get the Inspector? . . . He's taking his time . . . Yes, it is that! . . . It's the last thing I expected on my patrol. There was no struggle . . . Everything as tidy as if she was serving tea—not a thing out of place—and a big black cat that's guarding the body . . . Gives you a creepy feeling—like she was alive and watching too . . ."

Clancy's words hit me head-on. That was it—"like she was alive and watching." As though this were just another of her eccentric forms of entertainment. As though she had made herself comfortable in the curved-back chair, tied her scarf tighter than usual, called Beauty, and settled back for a nap. That might be it—she could have been taking a nap when somebody sneaked up and . . .

Clancy clutched my arm. We saw her hand settle gently on the cat's back. Beauty snarled the way he always did when she started to brush his coat—a warning snarl that he didn't want to be disturbed.

Fortunately the police came then. Clancy introduced me to Inspector Green. He might have been an instructor of physics or mathematics at Tech, well tailored, serious and efficient. He had his crew of homicide specialists with him. There were also men in uniform from the regular police department. They didn't lose any time—when the flash bulb went off Beauty jumped down with a snarl and disappeared.

Clancy gave what information he had, including our names and what he knew about us. The Inspector's eyes rested only casually on me when Clancy said I had found the body, and had locked a suspect in an upper room.

Now that the authorities had taken over, I said, "My wife's pretty shaken, finding Mrs. Selton like this . . . Could I go up to her now?"

His voice was chilly. "I thought you found the body?"

It was strange that I had sensed no discrepancy when Clancy made his statement. If you are alone when you find a murdered person it will seem to you that you have made the first discovery. I felt like a molecule the Inspector was drawing with his magnet. "My wife came down to pay the rent . . . we always did on Saturday night . . . She was hysterical when she came back, in a few minutes. I came down to call the police."

Why on earth does a person fumble when he has nothing to hide? I hated to have to bring Lita's name into it. Subconsciously I was afraid. I cursed my own stupidity in having let Lita come down as I saw the stenographer making the cryptic hooks that would later be evidence in a murder trial.

The Inspector said for me to remain—my wife would join me soon. Almost immediately he had the lights turned back to the one rose-shaded bulb—I presume to have everything just as the murderer had left it. He nodded to one of his men and addressed Clancy. "Have Mrs. Redfern come down." I watched the detective follow Clancy upstairs. He would probably search our rooms. Well, let him!

My eyes searched for Lita's face as I heard her steps beside Clancy's. She was calm. There was nothing to show that she had gone to pieces but a short time ago. Time? My God, it seemed like years. There's no such thing as time. Her hand reached for mine as she came to stand beside me.

The Inspector said, "Was everything just as it is now when you discovered the body, Mrs. Redfern?"

Lita looked at the back of the chair, then around the room. "Yes, it was."

"Come over here in front. She won't hurt you, now. She's dead." His words were so coolly insolent that I found myself cursing under my breath. Lita's fingers gripped mine in a nervous spasm before she dropped my hand and stepped forward. She faltered once, then walked slowly to stand in front of the corpse. "It's just the same," she said, her voice rising to a sob.

When she was back, her cold hand in mine, I stared at the Inspector. How the devil could he be so cruel when he appeared so suave, so civilized? He looked almost friendly until he nailed you with those blue-grey eyes, like shafts of steel. His cultured Boston accent was delightful until he used it to insult you.

A man with the usual doctor's bag came in. "Sorry I'm

late. They sent me on a wild goose chase down by Lever Brothers." I knew he was the medical examiner when he went directly to the body. He picked up her hand and let it drop. I turned away as he peered down close to her face and throat. Lita rested her head on my shoulder. I put my arm around her. Poor child, this wasn't easy for her.

"How long has it been, Doctor?" Inspector Green asked.

"Not more than one, possibly two hours. Body not entirely cool yet. Rigor mortis hasn't set in. I can tell more accurately after I have examined the stomach contents and the blood. How soon can I have it?" He looked up brightly, almost ghoulishly, it seemed to me. Mrs. Selton had already lost her identity. She was a body to be worked on—her last meal examined, her fingernails to see if they held fragments of her murderer. It wasn't true—she wasn't dead. She would move soon. We would see her again caressing her smoky Persian, putting this Inspector in his place . . .

His clipped words demanded, "What time was it when you came downstairs, Mrs. Redfern?"

The doctor was going out the door. I dreaded seeing him go because the searchlight was thrown on us. The thought of Lita's earring in my pocket made me uneasy. But how would he know where I had picked it up?

Lita was looking vaguely back at the Inspector. I tried to help her. "Remember the Pops Concert was over."

"Let her speak for herself."

"Why, yes, that was it," Lita said. "It was only a little after nine-thirty. Miss Brundage left for her apartment and I came down here to pay the rent."

He kept looking at his wrist watch. "It is ten fourteen now." As he said it, his eyes picked up Lita again. "That would be just under an hour." The doctor's words rang in my ears: "Not more than one, possibly two." He was being safe. He would narrow it down later.

"Wasn't that a strange time to pay your rent?"

Lita's words, low and unconvincing. "She liked us to pay on Saturday. I thought there might be a big row if we didn't."

He smiled then, a smile without a trace of warmth. "You had a great many rows?"

"No. That is, they never meant anything. She wouldn't have let us stay if she hadn't wanted us." Lita was becoming indignant. I pressed her hand.

He turned to me. "And when did you first see the body, Mr. Redfern?"

"I came down as soon as I knew about it."

"Your call came in at nine-fifty-seven."

I was stunned. Surely it had been more than seventeen minutes since I had phoned the division? But that wasn't what the Inspector was interested in. He wanted to know what I had done between nine-thirty and nine-fifty-seven. I managed to look him in the eye. "Naturally my wife was shocked by her discovery. It took her a while to calm down sufficiently to tell me about it. Surely you understand how that would be?"

Lita's fingers were cold, ice cold, as they lay so still in mine. I kept thinking that her fingers were as cold as the Inspector's eyes, but her heart was warmer. She spoke impulsively. "It was my fault, Inspector. I didn't tell him right away because I didn't want him to get mixed up in it. I saw it was murder and I knew you'd be suspicious —and you are!" Her voice broke and dry sobs echoed through the high rooms with the false rosy light and smell of death. If only Lita wouldn't get impulsive and say things!

The Inspector was patting himself on the back. You could see it in his eyes, in the controlled twitch of his lip. He spoke quietly. "Clancy, bring down your Number One suspect." Clancy ignored the sarcasm. He brushed Lita's arm as he passed and I knew he was trying to give her moral support.

We stood like two errant schoolchildren while the Inspector tapped his fingers on a marble-topped table and stared at the lace window curtains. I soon heard the stumbling feet of the strange man and Clancy's reassuring voice, "Easy does it. Quit taking the name of the Lord in vain. You ain't been torpedoed, if you did get a mite wet. The steps ain't hitting you in the face. That's just your imagination."

"A hell of a way to wake a man up."

"A little water never hurt nobody, or so they tell me."

Clancy left him inside the drawing-room and handed Green some papers. The man stood there and glared at the policemen and us, his large hands hanging limp. "What the hell is this?"

"Your name, please."

"Phillips—Bill Phillips. Who the hell are you?"

"I'm Inspector Green of the Cambridge Homicide Division. Keep a civil tongue in your head and answer the questions. How do you happen to be here?"

His bleary eyes were raised belligerently to the Inspector. "Why shouldn't I be here? Why all the questions? At sea it's the dirty subs and the goddam planes. Here it's questions. Why can't I sleep? I paid for my room."

The Inspector had made a quick survey of his papers. "When did you get off your ship?"

"Two—three days ago."

"You came here—to this house? Why?"

Phillips glanced up quickly at him and evidently decided he had nothing to fear from such a gentleman. "Ah, I was going by and the old lady askd me what I did and I told her. And she asked me about the subs and I told her. Then she offered me a room and I gave her five dollars. I had two—three hundred dollars. Why not?"

I wondered if he was telling the truth. As eccentric as Mrs. Selton was, I hardly thought she would take a man of that type into her home. And certainly not if he were drinking. He might have been the one she was arguing with. And he—

"I didn't want the room. But I couldn't keep her off my mind, so tonight I came back and went up to bed. You can ask her."

"You better ask her."

Phillips looked at him and then moved slowly over to the upright corpse. He didn't flinch but he backed away, inch by inch. His hand brushed quickly across his mouth. "She's been done in."

"Yes. And you did it, Phillips." I was to hear the Inspector say that several times, but each time it came to me as a distinct shock. He made each statement believable. "You were drunk and she ordered you out and you snapped the silk about her neck and tied it as you make fast a line at sea."

"What the hell? I didn't do the old dame in. Never saw her but the once. She was like a blooming petunia out there in the yard. Why all the fuss? Bury her. I've seen enough corpses in the last year, young ones, shark bait . . ."

He backed away as Beauty came yowling into the room, the cat's wild eyes resenting all of us. "I didn't do it, I tell you. Ask him." He pointed at me. "He saw me come in."

"I didn't see you come in. And I didn't hear you."

His jaw sprung into action, "You was too busy. Down on all fours. Jeez! You had just done it!" He looked from me to the distorted features of the corpse and then to the Inspector, "If I'da known, I'da backed out of here in no time! She was dead then. I wondered why he was shouting and her sitting right there!"

Dammit, I couldn't keep my body from trembling. I

wanted to bash his face in. The Inspector was watching me with mild amusement. "What were you doing on the floor, Redfern?"

Phillips cut in, "He jumped like he was shot when he heard me behind him and he stuffed something in his pocket."

I could feel Lita's fingers tighten on mine. And I could feel her earring—the one with the blue stone that I had once mended—sharp against the lining of my pocket. In a moment I would have to show it to the Inspector. It would link Lita to the murder of Mrs. Selton. There was no evidence now—just the time element—but the earring would be a tangible piece of evidence. If it were only something of mine.

The Inspector barked, "Well?"

My hand went into my pocket. I searched the Inspector's face. How could I tell him that Lita never hurt anything in her life—that she made me let the mice loose that we caught in the wastebasket? I always had to carry them to the park. My fingers felt past the paper to the earring. I started to draw it out past the paper. The paper? I found that under the chair. Hurriedly, before the Inspector could assist me, I pulled that out.

Something was written on it. Before I could smooth it out enough to read, the Inspector tore it from my grasp. He frowned. Then he read very distinctly, "The Stroke of Death. May it forever part our ways."

CHAPTER FOUR

"WHAT DOES this mean?" The Inspector was impatient as though I had tricked him.

"I don't know."

His sharp staccato voice, "You don't know? You hid it. You jumped when you heard somebody."

"Who wouldn't? I reached down to pick this off the floor. I hadn't heard anyone come in. Then I knew somebody was there, right behind me—it might be the murderer. Why shouldn't I jump back?"

He viewed me with positive distaste and spoke flatly to Clancy. "Bring down the ladies."

"While we're waiting, Mr. Redfern, you can come over here and turn out your pockets."

It's strange what a difference a few minutes can make. None of the articles in my pockets had any significance now, not even the earring. But I was glad my back was to Lita. She need never know that she had dropped her earring as she bent over Mrs. Selton.

I laid them out on the marble-topped table—handkerchief, trick knife as seen in *Esquire,* book of matches, crumpled pack of cigarettes, one blue stone earring and some small change. I let the small flakes of tobacco and the dust particles fall to the carpet as I displayed the empty pockets.

He waved a disinterested hand. "Put them back." But I was sure that he could have told me the serial number of the knife, also that I was by nature impetuous because the cigarettes had been ruthlessly torn into.

I was able to smile as Lita put her small hand back in mine when I returned to my place in the drawing-room entrance. The old gals were carrying on like a couple of awakened birds, "Carrie gets more inconsiderate every day. I thought we were not going to have a soiree." Brundage was doing the whining.

"And strange policemen!" Miss Lovelace said, "She knows I don't care for them. She knows how they treated me when I drove my electric. I did not like to run over them, but it was almost impossible to avoid them. You remember that time they drove me into Filene's Automatic waving their aims?"

Brundage snapped, "I was in the seat beside you! They shouldn't be invited to our soirees—they have a nice building of their own."

I almost chuckled as I looked at the Inspector—he was

registering cultured patience. Then I thought of the poor old ladies and of what was in store for them. I turned to look at them, picking their way down the carpeted stair, with Clancy solemn, in their wake. Neither was her usual neatly-packaged self. Lovelace had on a mauve silk, the hem of her nightgown trailing beneath. She had on white gloves and a white lace fascinator over her curls. Brundage was encased in a faded silk robe, a God-awful baby-blue night cap atop her sour face and spotless white gloves on her hands.

They had come to the bottom step and stood for a moment surveying us imperiously. Lovelace knew it first. She gave a piercing scream just as she stepped away from the stairs. Brundage, always slower, stumbled into the drawing-room. She made straight for the corpse. "Carrie!"

I felt a lump rise in my throat as I watched the pathetic creature, her jaw slack, her face contorting. Lovelace walked stiffly into the room to join her. When Brundage started to whimper, Lovelace led her gently to a love seat.

They were as frightened as two doves on a straw staring into the hooded head of a cobra. They didn't seem aware that they sat where they always sat at the Saturday night soirees, facing a corpse. I felt indignantly that the Inspector might have warned them. His ghoulish sense of the dramatic was in the poorest taste.

He spoke gently, for him, "Your name is Lovelace?"

Even at such a time she couldn't hide her pride of family.

"It is Miss Evelyn Lovelace!"

"When did you last see Mrs. Selton?"

"She had tea with us this afternoon."

"What time was that?"

She looked sharply at him, "At four, of course. We always have tea at four."

Brundage came to life. "It was four-thirty, don't you remember, Evelyn? You were late. You went out for some scones and I thought you would never return. Carrie was frightfully nervous. She kept jumping up and looking out the window . . ."

"That isn't important," the Inspector stated. "Did you see her after that, Miss Lovelace?"

"I saw her from the stairwell when she was quarrelling with her granddaughter."

"That's right!" Brundage exclaimed, "We did see her then." She gave a furtive glance at the distorted features of the once nervous Carrie. "It was frightful—that bitter quarrel!"

"We'll come to that later," the Inspector admonished. "I want the time *now*."

"It must have been about seven-thirty."

Brundage corrected her, "It was closer to eight. I should think you would remember, Evelyn. The cuckoo sang eight times just as we went back into our rooms. You said you felt a migraine attack coming on and said you wished to retire. I told you then that I couldn't possibly go to sleep so early."

Miss Lovelace closed her eyes and didn't answer. Brundage must have been hard to put up with.

"Was that the last time you saw the deceased, Miss Brundage?"

At the word, "deceased," her eyes jerked to her old friend. I had a horrible feeling that she was about to howl. She clicked her teeth and looked wildly at the Inspector. "Yes, it was. I heard her talking though." She pointed to me. "He can tell you. I was in their rooms. They were both asleep, their radio blasting the roof. As much as Evelyn has had to put up with—having a room next to them, she could not put up with that noise. She asked me to speak to them. And also to go down to Carrie's for some aspirin."

"Did you—that is, come down for the aspirin?"

"No. Mrs. Redfern gave me a bottle and told me that I would not have to go."

"She insisted you not go down?"

Brundage's head snapped in her effort to scrutinize Lita. "Yes, she did! Oh. . . . Oh!" She held her bosom up and stared open-mouthed at us. That thick skull of hers had jumped to a conclusion.

The Inspector could afford to wait—with us. "You heard her talking—to whom?"

Miss Brundage was still keeping us in view. "To George, the furnace boy."

Lita jumped in, "George and Carol went for a walk. I don't think they were any place near."

"You said so yourself. You said, 'Is she turning *them* out into the storm? After that the door slammed."

"That was simply because I was worried about them. I resent your insinuating that George had anything to do with this crime. George is a fine young man."

"You ought to know—you were kind enough to him!" Brundage could be as spiteful as a tabby-cat when the mood suited her. Clancy, God love him, walked sternly over to Lita's side, and gave Brundage the benefit of his glowering countenance. The Inspector had the faint end of a smile on his lips. I began to understand why he staged his investigation in this dramatic manner—the clashes of personalities told him a great deal—and he wasn't one to miss anything.

He turned very calmly to Lovelace. "What was your impression of the voices in the drawing-room when Miss Brundage left to get the aspirin?"

"I didn't hear any. My head was throbbing. One doesn't hear anything when their radio is on."

I knew that Lita was going to reply before she did. Her fingers dug into mine. But her voice was surprisingly cool, "Your rooms are so much closer to the drawing-room than ours, Miss Lovelace, that you must have heard the voices after our radio was turned off. As far down the hall as we are, we could hear the voices and the slam of the door at the close of the conversation."

"My dear girl! Your interest in the household's recent pandemonium far exceeds mine. I had heard all of the bickering I could tolerate." Aware then, possibly by the look on Lita's face, that she had hurt her, she said, "Forgive me! I truly meant no offense." She raised a gloved hand to adjust the white fascinator. "This migraine would descend on me just when I needed all of my powers of resistance."

Beauty howled pitifully at that moment, as though in sympathy. Lovelace reached down to comfort him and the little beast became a black ball of fury. He spat and struck at her with his sharp claws. Had it not been for the white gloves I'm sure he would have torn her hand. Clancy was so outraged, he sent the cat flying with his wrathful, "Scat!"

Poor Miss Lovelace was trembling, her well-shaped hands, large for a woman of her size, fluttering like helpless leaves. The Inspector chose not to spare her. "Tell me, Miss Lovelace, of some of this 'recent pandemonium.' "

Her hands quieted and she drew a long, struggling breath. "I should say that this recent condition had its inception in the appearance of the granddaughter, Caroline. Naturally, it was a shock to Carrie, never too stable emotionally, to have this girl come unannounced. All of the old griefs that had been quiescent for so many years again confronted her. Since the daughter's cruel departure, Carrie had not had a word from her."

"What makes you so sure Mrs. Selton hadn't heard?"

Lovelace didn't speak. She seemed pondering this, when Brundage, impatient of such niceties, informed the Inspector, "She told us often enough! Always parading her grief. She couldn't believe that a daughter could be so heartless. Then when this daughter's daughter worms her way into the house—" she glanced significantly at the Inspector— "she came from Washington and brazenly admitted she was in trouble—instead of sending her packing, Carrie tries the same methods she tried with the mother—tries to make a lady of her."

The Inspector held up his hand but there was no stopping Brundage now that she was having her say. She looked more like a shrunken pudding bag than a pudding now—her face tan and wrinkled. "Today at tea she hardly made sense. And Evelyn late with the scones! It was all I could do to keep my head. She kept saying, 'Tonight is the night! I wonder if it will work!' She kept calling on all those papist saints that I hadn't heard her mention in years. I offered to read one of my original poems. She was most insulting." She sent an offended look at the poor corpse and hurried on, "She said, 'Bother your poems, Amy! Why don't you save scrap paper?' But this much I can tell you, she was afraid—she was afraid she was going to die tonight!"

She was a Cassandra who had arrived too late. But she brought the same effects with her—the heavy sense of doom, the inevitability of violence and death. There was the scent of decay in that room with its murky light, its dusty hangings, and close air.

I was glad to hear the gentle voice of Miss Lovelace,

"Carrie was afraid. She feared someone. But above all, she feared for Caroline—feared that she would throw away her life as her mother had done. She meant to be firm, to have a—"

Brundage's white-gloved hands clapped together. ". . . A show-down! That's what Mrs. Redfern said!" Her small eyes made the rounds before settling on Lita. "You said it was time to have a show-down when Carrie was trying to put some sense into that Caroline's head. You would have gone right down then and—" she glanced triumphantly at the corpse—"if your husband had not held you back until later."

It was Lita who sensibly kept me from giving a public display of homicide. She answered with one clear word, "Rubbish!"

"You hated Carrie. Did you or did you not accuse your benefactor of snooping into your belongings? Snooping was the word I am sure you used. Why you should feel that anything you possessed would be of interest to the widow of a member of the New England Watch and Ward Society is beyond my comprehension . . ."

The Inspector raised a determined hand. "You can tell me later, Miss Brundage. Our time is short."

"Well, she did so accuse her. If you really want to get at the bottom of this murder, yqu want the facts. She also made Carrie cry by saying that she deliberately let Beauty in to eat that filthy bird. And she said that Beauty should be done away with!"

Hearing only his name and not understanding how close to death he had come, Beauty came running to her. He seemed about to jump on her lap when her foot shot out. "Shoo! Get away!" That set the creature to howling and padding about the room.

The Inspector got control again. "Bring down the doctor."

It struck me then as strange that Dr. Oglesbie hadn't been down before. Surely he had heard the commotion. Whatever else he was, he was not a stupid man. It shocked me to hear him joking with Clancy, "Well, this promises to be good! So, you're in on it tonight too, Clancy—one of our little meetings. I promise you anything is likely to happen!" His small chucklings hit us like a spray of ice. He lowered his voice to a stage whisper. "Sometimes it's a bit dull, but tonight, I have an idea—"

Something was wrong. His sharp eyes took us all in. I could tell that he was uneasy, although he bowed carefully to the maiden ladies, to the room in general, gave me a casual nod and bestowed a smile and deep bow on Lita. He was nervous. "We seem to have a great many uniforms here tonight. Reminds me of the time we had the Scollay Square crowd here." His laugh held the cynical note that was so much a part of him. He waved a small, immaculate hand. "If you gentlemen of the Division will pardon the comparison."

Standing there in the dim light, falsely jovial against our sombre background, his personality stood out like a white etching on black. The clipped Vandyke, red against his pale skin, small even teeth between the red lips. He had a soft white shirt open at the throat, long-sleeved, fastidiously cuff-linked. Tan slacks carefully creased. Woven house shoes. I knew then why I had always instinctively detested him. There was no doubt but that his appetites were masculine, but he was too fastidious, too nicey-nice. Every move he made seemed to be false. I distrusted him.

He smiled urbanely. "Are you playing tableaux? And did I interrupt? Or was Clancy sent to find a spider— one of those scavenger hunts?"

"We're not playing a game, Dr. Oglesbie. We're in deadly earnest. What did you do from six o'clock on this evening?"

The doctor took out a spotless handkerchief and wiped his hands. "I certainly don't like your tone. I might ask, what business is it of yours?"

The Inspector turned back his coat, his eyes never leaving Dr. Oglesbie's face. More frantic wiping of his hands while the good doctor stared back, the starch gone from him, meekness in its place. "I was in my room. I never left it. As you have doubtless heard, I am an anthropologist. At present I am engaged on my magnum opus, a study of the skeletal differences of the, let us say—" he waved a soft hand in the direction of the maiden ladies, his meekness melted away under his egotistical fire— "members of the New England Historical and Genealogical

Society and the immigrant who has spent but a short time on our hospitable shore."

The ladies fluffed their garments about their virginal frames and stared in fascinated horror at the doctor. The Inspector remarked dryly, "I am familiar with Dr. Hrdlicka's works."

Oglesbie had the grace to look abashed. "Oh, so you are familiar with Ales' work? Good old Ales! A very remarkable man.

"Well, as I was saying—I didn't leave my room. Mrs. Selton, knowing how engrossed I am apt to be, had Caroline bring a tray to my room. It was delicious—breadcrumb dumplings with the beef stew tonight—I complimented Caroline on her culinary achievement . . ."

I wondered if he was some sort of a monster—that he could speak of food, with his hostess sitting there, the life choked out of her—the bread dumplings he was smacking his lips over, soggy in—God! How much longer was the Inspector going to stand there, his face placid, his eyes watching the doctor before he decided to impale him? I felt the sweat trickling down from my brow.

There was a wicked gleam in the Inspector's eyes as he asked, "What did Mrs. Selton say when you thanked her for the dumplings?"

Dr. Oglesbie wet his lips before speaking. "I haven't had that opportunity."

The twinkle went out of the eyes. "Well, you have it now. I'm sure she would like to hear your compliments before we proceed."

The doctor was visibly ill at ease. Whether that was guilt on his face or not I couldn't tell. Perhaps the Inspector knew. I watched the doctor finally lean forward in his most gallant manner, "Mrs. Selton, may I say—"

He froze. I had never seen a man freeze before—from emotional shock. If he was putting on an act, it was the best piece of acting I had ever witnessed. I would have sworn right then that that was the first he knew of Mrs. Selton's death. The blood left his lips until they were the same color as the exposed teeth. The peaked Vandyke, tipped so archly forward, turned to stone. That was the appearance with his rigid pose.

The hands came to life first, rubbing, rubbing. He straightened stiffly. "Good God! Who did it?" The sinister gaze of the Inspector sent him into hysterical outbursts. "You don't think? God! You don't believe? You can't . . ." He stumbled over to an ancient chair and sat down. I wiped my own face as though I had gone through torture. I wouldn't have blamed the doctor if he had gone out and cut his throat—the Inspector was either a very smart psychologist or a damned sadist. Still, if Dr. Oglesbie had strangled that helpless old woman . . .

Carol and George were catapulted into the room from the back entrance, an officer at their heels. "I found these two skulking through the shrubbery. They peeked into the front windows, then ran around to the back. I caught them before they got away."

Carol was indignantly facing the officer, her back to us. "You are certainly not a gentleman! We were not trying to get away. This is where we live."

The Inspector had of course been taking in the newcomers. He spoke casually. "Do you always peek in the windows, then run around through the bushes?"

Carol turned on him, her dark-fringed eyes as imperious as only young frightened loveliness has a right to be. Bright drops of moisture clung to her jet-black hair, like sequins on dark fringe. "No, we don't! You're insulting. Grandmother has no right to . . ."

Her flashing eyes swept to her grandmother. George must have seen it about the same time. His umbrella clattered to the floor and he stepped forward to hold Carol. She strained at his hands like a wild thing. I could hear somebody sobbing—I discovered it was Lita. Carol was screaming in a thin voice, "Let me go! Let me go! Grandmother!"

Then she was on her knees, her head buried in her grandmother's lap. "Grandmother! Grandmother! Oh, why did you do it? Please, please, Grandmother, you could have stopped me. I didn't think you loved me." She was sobbing uncontrollably.

Then something happened that none of us was prepared for. It happened with a suddenness that left us all dumb. During her lifetime Mrs. Selton had been unable to show the slightest touch of tenderness to Carol. She made the girl, who had never done even the most casual of household tasks, do all the scrubbing and the cooking and the cleaning. Her sharp tongue constantly lashed at her—to hurl a final insult almost with her last breath.

Now in death with the girl sobbing on her knees before her, the old lady bent forward as though in soft benediction.

Before our startled eyes—the corpse fell forward, the lifeless head resting, the blood-red scarf sprawling over the young girl's dusky hair.

CHAPTER FIVE

WE WERE HERDED into the dining-room after that and the big double doors into the drawing-room closed. They were moving her out—I could hear the heavy shuffling. Mrs. Selton, whose voice had been so often raised in anger through the tapestried rooms, was leaving this house to which she had come in happiness.

Carol was still sobbing, her eyes closed against the sodden wisp of handkerchief. George was standing white-faced behind her and Lita was havering over her chair. The rest of us stood around, pathetically inadequate.

"There are a few more details before you can be sent to your rooms," the Inspector said.

Dr. Oglesbie asked the question that was possibly in all our minds, "Are we to understand that we will be detained in our rooms—for this murder with which we had nothing to do?"

The Inspector looked bored. "As yet there is not sufficient evidence to detain you."

I'm sure he meant it as a collective you because he was
occupied in studying the slip I had found under the chair,
but the doctor took it as a personal affront. His lips were
trembling and his small eyes mulish when Carol startled
him by exclaiming, "Murder? Did somebody murder
Grandmother? I thought . . ."

The Inspector gave her a sharp look before going on
with his paper inspection. Seeing her grandmother in her
usual chair, the same scarf around her throat, only tighter,
it was possible that she thought the strong-minded woman
had done it herself. It would not be easy for her to imagine
anybody getting the best of her grandmother.

Carol spoke again. "Did Grandmother have a talk with
you tonight, Dr. Oglesbie?"

We all looked at her, especially the doctor. "Of course
not! I did not see her."

Her voice, high with tension, moved bravely on. "She
said she was going to. I told her, you see, that you had—
had grabbed me . . ."

"Caroline!" It was a cry of agony. "Think of the implica-
tion of your words!" He was trembling and I didn't blame
him. George moved toward him—his fists clenched. The
Inspector stepped between them. "This is no time for
minor dramatics." He pushed George back and addressed
Carol. "So the doctor made passes at you when you carried

up his tray and you reported the incident to your grandmother? Or was it more than passes?"

Carol's face flooded with color, "I don't—no—no—that was all." She seemed to regret that she had spoken.

"What was your grandmother's reaction? Just exactly what did she say?"

Carol showed her embarrassment. "She said—at first she said that if I were a nice girl, men wouldn't bother me. Then she got angry and said she would speak to him."

The Inspector let Oglesbie writhe. He was scrutinizing George—poor George, whose face was a cloud of anger as he surveyed Oglesbie. You didn't have to be Inspector Green to know what George was thinking.

George was handed a sheet of paper by the Inspector. "Write this sentence, 'The Stroke of Death. May it forever part our ways.'" George stared dumbly at him and then at me. I grinned. George shrugged his shoulders and wrote. Although he was almost a Harvard graduate, he kept making mistakes and trying to erase. The Inspector became annoyed. "Just scratch it off and go on."

It was next handed to Carol. She had started crying again. Maybe it was the word, "Death." Tears kept dropping on the sheet of note paper. Finally she handed it to Miss Lovelace. Lovelace, always proud of her handwriting and impatient of the modern disinterest in penmanship, wrote the words with a fine, free flourish. Brundage had considerable skill but she couldn't seem to remember the words. "Will you repeat it again, Inspector?"

"Copy it—the words are there—or can't you read them?"

"I haven't my spectacles, if you must know!" she snapped.

He repeated the words again until they drummed against my brain like the message of a savage tribe. What could they mean? Or did they mean anything? Was it just a red herring to put the police off the scent? But why would the murderer leave a sample of his handwriting? It would have to be somebody unfamiliar with modern police methods.

Phillips? He was cursing under his breath as the paper was handed him. He wrote laboriously in a heavy hand, consigning to hell all the tomfoolery that landlubbers thought of. He should have taken a ship right out. The damned so and so's who wouldn't let him alone.

He tossed it scornfully to Oglesbie. The doctor was almost too nervous to write. He tried to laugh it off. "If an expert can relate this to my normal scrip, he will have to be an expert."

"He will be," the Inspector remarked succinctly.

Lita was next. I saw the Inspector watching her closely as she wrote the words without faltering. I followed.

The Inspector folded the paper and put it in his pocket. Miss Lovelace appealed to him, "Inspector! Could Miss Brundage and I be excused? I have been ill all evening. Surely, whatever you have in store for us can wait until morning." She did look drawn enough to touch even the heart of the efficient Green. I was wrong, though. He had no heart.

He gazed calmly down on her fragile Brahmin features, "A few more questions. Then fingerprinting."

She groaned, and Brundage pursed her lips at him.

"We were discussing the animosities that flourished in the house. Could you give us a bit more of the particulars, Miss Lovelace?"

She sighed and folded her hands in resignation. "I mentioned the trouble between Caroline and her grand-mother. That went on from the time she stepped into the drawing-room—until her grandmother was stopped by death."

Carol interrupted fiercely, "Grandmother loved me. She just didn't know how to show it. And you didn't help any —you and Miss Brundage! I could have won her over— I know I could have—if I'd had time."

Lovelace didn't let this outburst disturb her, nor the tears that followed. She spoke only to the Inspector. "You asked me and I shall give the facts as I saw them. Until the Redferns arrived, George was docile, if not very ambitious or efficient. Under Mrs. Redfern's influence he became unruly and noncooperative."

Miss Brundage pulled the dissection down to her own morbid level. "He was surly and—and vicious! Did you see that look he gave Carrie before he went out the door?" Her sour gaze sought him out. "That was the last time we saw her alive!"

We were all speechless. More so than the brace of ducks

hanging so limply on the oiled canvas, mute testimony of the gastronomic avidity of the Seltons. George looked more helpless than they.

But she wasn't finished with her cutting. "You might be interested to know that Carrie was forced to bring Mrs. Redfern's attention to the fact that she should not entertain George in her rooms in her husband's absence—especially en déshabille!"

I'm afraid I would have laughed aloud if the same impulse hadn't overtaken Lita. She hid her head on my shoulders, her body shaken with hysterical merriment. I put my handkerchief over her face—this was no time for laughter. Controlling my own features, I looked at Carol. The little fool was furious. She was eaten up with jealousy. A fine kettle of fish!

Even Lita didn't laugh long, though. Brundage plunged her verbal knife in deep. "It was because of this interest, I presume, that just before George went out the door— that last time we saw Carrie—Mrs. Redfern declaimed, 'That old lady ought to be choked!'"

Lita's hysteria vanished under this shock. I could feel her body still and suddenly cold under my touch. That bitch! That old bitch! She had more venom in her system than a dozen cancerous patients. It wasn't easy for me to speak to the Inspector without first blasting her. "May I say, Inspector, that my wife is accustomed to using such expletives. She has always used them and she has difficulty even stepping on a bug."

I should have maintained a dignified silence, or at any rate kept my mouth shut. There was a half-smile on the Inspector's face. "Yes, you may say it."

We were all jittery when it came to the fingerprinting, even Lovelace and Brundage. Lovelace, probably because of soiling her harp-playing fingers. Brundage was more explicit. "This is preposterous! I resent being treated like a criminal. You have the murderers in this room. Why don't you take them away and leave the respectable people in peace?"

The Inspector reminded her, "We mustn't hurry through this, Miss Brundage. I assure you the murderers, since you imply there are more than one, won't get away."

He turned from this gentle speech to the interrogation of George. "What did you do between the time you were seen going out the door and your hesitant return?"

"Carol and I took a walk."

The Inspector smiled. "It wasn't very good walking weather, was it? Or didn't you notice?"

"We didn't care."

"Where did you walk? Did you notice?"

"Yes, sir. We walked down Brattle until we came to Craigie Street. Then down Concord Avenue to the Common. We walked around the Common and then over to the Yard . . ."

"Does Harvard Yard make a pleasant rendezvous during a violent electric storm? Or didn't you know that trees are dangerous havens at such times?"

"We didn't care. We enjoyed the storm. We were pretty blue."

The Inspector seemed pleased at this admission. George was going to be almost too easy. I did wish that he would guard his admissions of emotional strain. I began to be afraid that he was walking straight toward a trap.

"If the testimony given so far is accurate, you were gone about three hours."

"I wouldn't know. It didn't seem very long. It wasn't long enough to convince Carol that she should run away with me." He was like a small boy spilling the bitterness from his heart. Carol gasped, "George!"

"Sorry."

"So you wanted to get out of Cambridge, fast. Why?"

"I wanted to get away. I hated it here. I love Carol and I wanted to take her to my folks. She wasn't happy either. I could work on the farm until I was called."

"She decided it would be smarter to remain?"

Carol answered, "I refused to go because I wanted to win my grandmother over first. I knew there was some love in her some place because she was my mother's mother, and there had to be! Then, too, she said that about my mother . . . I had to prove . . ."

"What did she say about your mother?"

Poor Carol looked frantically about the room. George moved closer to her, his lean frame bending solicitously. He couldn't help her, but Brundage did. "If you will pardon me, Inspector," she said primly, "Carrie told us what we already knew—that Caroline was a—a—" I hoped she'd choke, but no such good luck—"bastard!"

Caroline screamed at her, "It isn't true! It isn't true!" before bursting into helpless tears. George walked over to Brundage, his hands clenched, his scowl enough to terrify a stout heart, which Brundage hadn't. "Inspector! Inspector! Don't let him come . . ." After the Inspector had shoved George to one side, she quavered triumphantly, "You see what I mean, Inspector! That was his attitude toward Mrs. Selton."

The Inspector evidently saw—even more than he had expected to. He continued to question George. "Am I to understand that you stood the storm out in Harvard Yard, with the rain coming down in torrents?"

George was more than subdued after his burst of anger, "No, sir. We went into the Rathskeller—McBride's, until we came home."

"Until you came back to this house where you had been given asylum to peek in the windows to see if the crime had been discovered."

"No, sir. I mean I'm not in the habit of peeking in the windows, but we were afraid that Mrs. Selton might be angry . . ."

"And well she might! If she lived through it!" George wasn't rising to the Inspector's bait, not even when another choice lure to his anger was added. "We often get the guilty parties on their return to the scene. They seem helpless against their morbid curiosity."

The fingerprint expert was waiting for George—the rest of us had complied. In spite of Lovelace's urgent need for relaxation, she waited with Brundage for whatever unsolicited aid they could tender the arm of the law.

I was the next recipient of the Inspector's attention. "You said the door of your apartment was open during what may have been the murder interval. Do you wish to add that during that time you heard no struggle, no cry, nothing to indicate that Mrs. Selton was being deprived of her life?"

"I will add that."

He looked at me blandly, as though he were asking me to present a solution to a mathematical problem that was of no interest to anybody, least of all himself. But I wasn't deceived. He was maneuvering me into position so that he could strike. He was moving closer. The ends of my fingers began to feel numb.

"Had she made an outcry you could have heard it?"

"I'm sure I could have—during that time while our door was open."

Lita's tapered fingernails were pressing sharply against my fingers. The Inspector smiled at me. "You heard the door slam, ending the conversation with whomever she was speaking. It is your opinion that she was alive after this person or persons left?"

"Yes, it's my opinion, for what it's worth."

He nodded happily. "It's worth a great deal." I seemed to be his brightest pupil, clear up at the head of the class.

I looked him full in the eye, hoping he would not notice Lita's nervousness. If only she hadn't gone down to pay that damn rent!

"The door remained open and there was no outcry."

"I can swear to that, Inspector. I was in the room with them and you could have heard a pin drop throughout the house." Beauty, who had been let in and had been prowling around trying to find his mistress, took that moment to jump on Miss Brundage's lap shutting her off. He just about scared the liver out of her before she succeeded in driving him off and for a few seconds I was devoutly happy. Lovelace scolded her for not befriending the poor cat. "He's desolate, Amy, can't you see that?"

"Of course I can! But he never bothered with me when Carrie was alive, why should I put up with him now? He makes me think of her."

The Inspector asked her, "Do you know the exact time you got into your room, after leaving the Redfern apartment?"

"I can tell you within three minutes. I didn't hear the cuckoo when I opened our door. The room was dark but I could tell that Evelyn was comatose, so I tiptoed into my room and put on my bedside light. I was so grateful that she had found surcease from her headache in sleep. When the pain became intolerable, sometimes she would fall into that heavy slumber. I felt justified in reading a few minutes before I turned off my light."

"The time, Miss Brundage!" The Inspector had to work

for the information he got from her, "You were going to
tell us the time you entered your room."

"Oh, yes. If you would just give *me* time. I unpinned
my watch and wound it. The time was exactly nine-twenty-
eight."

"Would that coincide with your view, Mr. Redfern?"

"I would say that was approximately correct."

"How soon did your wife go downstairs?"

There was nothing for it but to tell the truth. I pressed
Lita's hand and said it: "It was probably five minutes."

He was pleased again. "Do you think that the murder
could have occurred and the murderer make his getaway in
five minutes?"

"It doesn't seem likely. Yet it would not take long for
a murderer to knot the scarf around her neck and hide . . ."

"That's what I think—it wouldn't take very long—not
over five minutes. When did your wife come back upstairs?"

I remembered that Lita did not return immediately. I
had smoked my cigarette—to the end, while I rinsed out
the glasses and the ale bottles. How long did that usually
take me? I knew I mustn't hesitate. "It couldn't have
been over five minutes or . . ."

Lita's hand relaxed, cold and still in mine, as the Inspector stopped me. "Correct! As you agree, five minutes
is ample time to snuff out a life—especially when the
murderer is young and strong and the victim old and weak.
Five minutes to knot the scarf around her neck!"

I felt a knot being tied around Lita's neck and mine. Lita was right—we should have stayed out of it.

George took out a cigarette. As the flash of the match struck the emotion-charged air, Brundage gave an ear-splitting scream.

We all jumped as though we had been shot. George stood there, the match in his hand, with Brundage pointing a black-smeared finger at him. She finally got out what she was trying to say. "He had an umbrella!"

So what? I thought, as George stood there, the flame reaching to his fingers. He jerked and shook out the flame, his eyes unfathomable as he returned Brundage's scrutiny.

"He had an umbrella when he came back. He did not have one when he left. We all saw him go out the door, Evelyn and I and the Redferns." She dropped her finger from its accusing level and pressed her hands together as she sought the attention of the Inspector. "I wouldn't have thought a thing about it if Mrs. Redfern had not drawn my notice to it. She said, 'She is driving them out in the storm!'" It would have been funny if it hadn't been so serious—her melodramatic version of Lita's solicitation. "She also said, 'It is raining dogs and cats. They did not have an umbrella. That is why they came back.'"

The Inspector asked Lita, "You admit you made those statements?"

Lita's voice was without expression. "Not those exact words and certainly not the manner—it is true in essence.

Please understand that I was only jumping to conclusions in presuming that she was talking to George. Something that Miss Brundage said . . ."

"I know. I said that Carrie said, 'Get out and stay out! Don't ever come in this house again!' She wasn't jumping to conclusions. We both knew it was George."

Lita spoke even more tiredly, "I prefer to state what I knew, Miss Brundage. I did not *know* it was George. I believe him when he said that they walked to Harvard Yard, stopped at McBride's, and then home. I firmly believe that Mrs. Selton was talking to somebody else, possibly a stranger to me, or perhaps somebody in this room who finds it more expedient to keep quiet."

The Inspector spoke. "What you believe is not of any importance, Mrs. Redfern. You are here only to tell the truth about what you did, what you saw and what you heard."

I saw the Inspector's head turn slowly in the direction of George. I watched him—I couldn't look at George. He was too much like a woolly lamb being led to the slaughter pens by a cynical old nanny. "So you came back?"

"Yes, sir."

His answer was so startling that I stared in amazement at him. Lita murmured, "Oh, Paul!"

I saw that Carol was holding on to her chair in an agony of apprehension, while the Inspector continued, "Mrs. Selton told you to get out?"

"No, sir."

"What did she say, then?" He was getting angry.

"Nothing, sir." I wished to God George would quit saying "sir" in that Eastern schoolboy manner. It sounded false. It sounded like hell. I didn't blame the Inspector for being annoyed.

"You mean to say you came back and she didn't say anything to you?"

"I didn't see her." He said it as though it wouldn't be believed, and it wasn't by anybody but Lita and me, and probably Carol. But the way she looked at him one couldn't tell. Didn't she know he'd come back?

"Perhaps you will tell us next that she was engaged in conversation with herself or some very convenient 'caller'?"

"No, sir. I didn't hear anything. I could hear the radio upstairs, that was all."

"Why did you come back?"

"To get an umbrella."

This was so weak. Especially after Brundage had forced him to say it.

"Why didn't you admit it—in the beginning?"

"I didn't think it was important, sir. It started to rain and I came back for an umbrella—that was all."

"You walked boldly in the front door, went up to your room without being intercepted by the lady of the house, got your umbrella and left?"

"No, sir, I came in the back door . . ."

"Oh, you sneaked in the back door. You were very quiet,

weren't you?"

"Yes, sir."

"Why?"

"I did not want Mrs. Selton to hear me."

"She did, though! And you walked in with your fists clenched and that scowl on your face and jerked the scarf about her throat!"

"Stop it!" Carol shouted. She had evidently made up her mind that George was guiltless, the victim of circumstances. I could only surmise what she thought, but it seemed to me that she was slow to help in his defense. But then, she couldn't know what he had actually done in the house. She was not so warm and impulsive as Lita.

"You can't say that!" she defied the Inspector. "I asked George to go after my umbrella and he did and that was all there was to it. He didn't want to go—he was afraid that Grandmother would say something."

The Inspector accepted the information Carol gave him but ignored her otherwise. "So you went to this girl's room! You knew Mrs. Selton wouldn't approve of that, didn't you?"

"If she saw me, she wouldn't. But I was very quiet."

"I have no doubt—no doubt at all."

Beauty had got back into the drawing-room—probably when the fingerprint man left. Alone now, he was howling like the lost soul of the dead woman. It sounded more terrifying than when he was in the room with us. Miss Brundage was right in that, at least—he seemed to be some part of Mrs. Selton, left behind.

The Inspector was thoughtfully inspecting the nail of his left index finger. He rubbed the cuticle tenderly as though he had discovered a slight redness that worried him. We all waited, not daring to move, hardly to breathe. Then he looked at Miss Brundage. "You heard the voice of the person to whom Mrs. Selton was speaking?"

She brightened. "I most certainly did."

"Had you ever heard the voice before?" He held up a detaining hand. "Think, now! Keep your emotions out of it. What you say may send somebody to the electric chair."

Her jaw dropped. Even she was impressed. But she didn't think very long—perhaps she wasn't capable of thinking. "I had heard the voice before, I could swear to that."

He bent his head to her, his eyes trying to force her to think back those hours to the time when Mrs. Selton could with violent voice order somebody from her house. "Could you positively identify that voice as belonging to somebody in this room?"

"I think it was George," she said.

It was time somebody spoke in George's defense. He didn't seem to care to. I said, "Inspector, I heard the voice, and had it been George's I would have recognized it."

Brundage refused to give up the limelight. "But, Mr. Redfern, there was the ale."

"What ale? Oh, for God's sake! You don't think I was

drunk?"

"You may not have known it, but intoxicating beverages have the ability, quite apart from one's own volition, to blunt the perceptions."

Clancy, who had been listening doggedly to the testimony, spoke up for the first time. "I can vouch for Mr. Redfern's holding two quarts of ale and its not affecting him at all. If he'd had as much as two quarts of Boston ale, I'd say he could hear the better for it."

The Inspector smiled briefly. He was spent for the time. And he hadn't been able to stick the label on one of us yet. "It will be better, Clancy, if we don't endorse any products. That's all for tonight."

CHAPTER SIX

CAROL WAS COOL at first to Lita's invitation to stay with us. You could see that she had changed toward Lita—the seeds the old gals had dropped were flourishing in receptive soil. But a backward glance at the closed doors of the drawing-room and the angry cat were enough to convince her that she better make the best of a bad bargain.

I marvelled at Lita's kindness in the face of Carol's ungraciousness. Carol slumped in a chair and refused to be drawn out. George stood about hardly knowing what to do. Lita put on the coffee and while I was in the bedroom she disappeared downstairs. When she came back she said she had been trying to get Beauty.

"He's all right; I don't see why you want to bother with everything." Of course, Carol meant that Lita was being too officious, but knowing Lita I wasn't surprised that she would think of the beast.

Lita brought the coffee in. Then she got up suddenly and went to the highboy. "They must have searched all our rooms. I don't see anything gone. Oh, yes, my white gloves."

"Why, Lita, you wouldn't know if your white gloves were gone. You never put them in the same place twice."

"Yes, I do, Paul. Several times I was almost late for my class, having to hunt for them." She smiled. "I made myself put them in the same spot. No matter how hard one tries to be careless, there are certain habits that are formed . . ."

"You sound just like Brundage in speech if not in spirit. Imagine that old grande dame telling the Inspector I was drunk. After I was so gallant to her . . ."

"That's what made her suspicious."

"Stop it, you two! I don't see how you can sit there and talk and talk . . ." She looked like a chunk of ice.

There was nothing for us to do but to humor her.

We finally got to bed, after George had left and Carol was comfortable on the horse-hair sofa. I wanted her to sleep in the bed with Lita but she refused. Lita cried a bit too after she was in my arms. We didn't talk about the murder—there was nothing to say. We had our thoughts, our questions, but we were too exhausted to discuss them. We were in a mess and we knew it.

I fell asleep. I woke up once with the sweat breaking

out on my body. Somebody was moving in the other room. I caught a glimpse of something white. But I fell asleep almost immediately. My dreams were worse than my waking moment. I saw Phillips, his face livid and cruel, strangling Mrs. Selton with his bare hands. I couldn't move to help her.

Something was tapping against my shoulder. I moved but the tapping continued. I opened my eyes and Carol was standing there in Lita's silk robe. She withdrew into the doorway, beckoning me and holding her finger to her lips.

Damn! I crawled out carefully and followed her. She closed the bedroom door. "Paul, will you come upstairs with me?"

Her face was flushed and her eyes too bright. "You've got a fever, Carol. Get back in bed."

"I'm all right." She stamped her slippered foot—Lita's slippers, too—her best ones. Carol hadn't been losing any time. "Listen to me, Paul. I have to go up in the attic."

"The attic?" I had been up there once when George asked me to help him bring down a heavy old chest for Carol to keep her clothes in. It was the only concession that her grandmother had made—after she had given Carol the money to pay her back room rent. "I suppose you can't wear that wispy dress all the time. I hope your clothes are worth it."

We almost broke our necks coming down the steep stairway. The attic itself was worse than any nightmare.

Churlish ancestors leered down from nails driven into the rough studs. They reigned over the decrepit, broken-down furniture on which the moths feasted, the padlocked chests and trunks, the dust and dirt in which the mice scurried, and the cobwebs over which the bats flitted. George and I could joke about it then, but even in midday it had its effect. In the middle of the night, right after a murder, and the murderer in all probability lurking about! Right then I heard Beauty yelp, and then a continuous fretful mewing.

"Look, Carol dear, we're all as nervous as cats. I know how you feel. You get in bed and I'll get the thermometer . . ."

Her look could have killed me. "Get this through your head, Paul: if you're not man enough to go with me, all right!"

"Why the attic?"

"My mother's letters are up there. I have to get them. You heard what that old—that old—" she preferred to think it and not say it—"woman said I was. Now, don't laugh!"

"You couldn't make me laugh now if you told an election story."

"Well, I saw my mother."

I gulped and looked around.

"Pay attention. I don't want Lita to wake up. She won't let you go."

I raised my voice at this happy thought. "Why don't

you get George?"

"Paul, that wouldn't be right. We're not married. These old gossips in this house."

"I have my reputation to consider."

She glared at me. "That's the thing I hate about you, Paul—everything's a joke to you."

"I might say I was never more serious. I'd like to go back to my wife."

"Go on, then." She ran toward the door. When I saw her open it into the hazy blue hall, I rushed over and grabbed her back and closed the door. "I'm very serious now. Talk fast."

"I dreamed that the letters were up there in Grand-mother's trunk. The letters Mother wrote when she was first married. She told me that Grandmother never answered. That always grieved her. When I opened my eyes and Mother was standing in this very room, I knew that it would be just as I dreamed. The police will be all over the place tomorrow and it will be too late. I'm not afraid to go up, are you, Paul?"

She couldn't be side-tracked—I could see that. She certainly inherited a big dose of stubbornness, even willful stubbornness. I lied bravely, "No, I'm not. I'll get my pants and a flashlight." She grabbed one of the bayberry candles off the highboy. "You're all right in your pajamas—it's not cold." She had me by the wrist and the door open. You know how a man feels without his pants. She said, "I have some matches," as she picked those up.

With one foot on the attic stairs, I stopped short. "Our door was locked. Did you unlock it?"

"I don't know. Come on." She was all excitement, like a pilgrim on a holy mission. I began to pray while she babbled, "I knew the door would be open. The trunk will be open too—you'll see."

I lighted the candle. Carol rushed forward. "Be careful, Carol! Do you want to break your neck?" My voice was so sharp that I must have been thinking about my own. I had difficulty following her. She was kneeling down before an open trunk. This was more than I had bargained for—the last time I had seen that attic, the door was locked, everything inside was locked.

"Here they are! Bring the candle closer. Yes, that's Mother's writing. Oh, Paul, I'll always be grateful to you!"

"Let's get the hell out of here now."

Before I could turn, the candle flame vanished. It went out like a light, leaving only the pungent smell of bayberry like a wraith. Carol whimpered. I wanted to help her but I couldn't move. Something was insinuating itself against my leg—it was moving on my bare feet.

Carol screamed. Stiff with fright as I was, I had to face it. I struck a match and lit the candle. Carol was staring up at me, her face white agains the blackness of her hair, her eyes enormous with fright. We both looked down. We went off into peals of laughter.

It was only Beauty, his back arched, his whole black

body replete with love. "The only time I ever saw him friendly—when he had a chance to scare us to death! Come on, Carol. Get Lita's robe out of that mess."

She got up and brushed herself off, "She'd have a fit if she knew."

"Oh, no, she wouldn't." Considering all the things she had worn of Lita's, I thought she ought to be at least grateful.

We made our way over to the door. I walked ahead holding the candle so Carol could see. Thank God, I could get back to bed. This business of prowling around in the dark, a dead mother clearing the way ahead of us, wasn't a healthy occupation.

"The door slammed—that's what blew out the candle—all easily explainable." I grabbed the knob. It turned but that was all. The door was locked—and on the outside!

"Open it, Paul. What's the matter?" I looked at her and she got the idea. "It's locked? But how . . ." Her voice trailed off.

I turned with the candle and looked stealthily about us. The murderer? He might be in the attic with the key in his pocket. The small flame illumined but a bare fraction of the big space. Shadows lay all about in nebulous shapes that expanded and contracted under the wavering light.

"Maybe the key dropped out, Paul, when the door slammed?" She was on her knees again feeling about the floor, her ribbon-tied letters in one hand. I had to deflate her feminine supposition. "The key would hardly turn in the lock before conveniently somersaulting."

She got up. "Paul, somebody locked us in."

I had to smile. "It's possible. Here, take the candle."
I hurled all of my strength against the old door and pulled
on the knob. They did their building well a century ago—
in the age when locksmiths laughed at love.

Carol was chattering nervously. "Somebody was in here
when we came, Paul. We frightened them away. Beauty
must have followed them." She began to whimper again.
"Maybe that was just a dream, Paul, and not my
mother . . ."

"It couldn't have been. The trouble was you just didn't
sleep long enough." I felt sorry at the forlorn look that
came over her. "If you'd slept longer, you see, you might
have discovered what we are supposed to do now."

"You're laughing, Paul. But, honestly, I saw my mother.
She was standing in white, by the highboy . . . I was so
frightened . . . When I looked again she was gone."

"You're right. Somebody was in the room." I picked up
a rickety old chair, heavy as a chest, and poised it. "That
somebody is having the run of the house right now. Our
door is unlocked. Lita is asleep . . ."

"Don't crash it, Paul! Please! George is right below
here." She picked up a heavy leg that had fallen off. "I'll
signal him. We don't want all those old people staring.
They'll think . . ." She was pounding out the signal, tap,
TAP TAP! "I used to do this with the broom handle on
the ceiling when Grandma took her nap . . . George always

answered."

I took the leg away from her and pounded the message with staccato brutality. It might mean, "I love you," but I was muttering something entirely different. I stopped to listen—no answer. "He's either dead, asleep, or gone."

"Knock the door down, Paul!" She wasn't waiting either. I might not be able to shatter the oak panels, but I could try. I picked up the chair again and raised it over my head. Just then the handle turned, hesitantly. Somebody was outside. I waited. The other person waited too. He would either finish us off or pretend innocence. The latter idea was the most tenable . . .

The knob turned again. I wanted to shout, "Open it! You damn fool!" I stood with the chair poised and whispered, "Get behind me, Carol." She moved in back, her body shaking so that the candlelight made the door and knob jerkily alive. The key was turning in the lock . . . it clicked back. Nothing happened. We were free to go. If I took my grasp from the chair to turn the knob I would be at a disadvantage . . .

The knob turned and the door came quietly open. I stood glaring into the strained but lovely face of Lita. I must have been the epitome of Gargantua—for a minute she looked terrified. Then her shoulders slumped in weariness. "Paul! Put that chair down!"

I complied, speechless. She was safe, and so was I. But I felt as though I had taken a beating. Carol came out from behind me, her face alight with pleasure. "Oh,

Lita!"

Lita's eyes swept over her and she turned to rush down the stairs. I called to her, "For God's sake, be careful!" I was right behind her, stopping only to give the chair a swing into the attic. I was in time to see Lita's body suddenly fly up, then go tumbling to the bottom.

The split second when the shock hit my brain—Lita! She must have thought . . . Lovely Lita with the dancing legs . . . Lita who moved too swiftly . . . did things too impulsively . . . her laughter . . . her endless kindness . . .

She lay so still—crumpled up into a soft heap. Phillips was moving toward her . . . He had something in his hands . . . something heavy . . . the stone cat!

CHAPTER SEVEN

ROARING AT HIM, I flung myself down the steps. Gently I picked Lita up in my arms. She was breathing—thank God! Not softly or rhythmically, but as though it hurt. I shouted, "Get a doctor—somebody!" I was carrying her into our rooms. Clancy stood in front of me. "Who did it? That guy?" He was prepared for Phillips. "No, Clancy, it was an accident. I don't know what Phillips had in mind but the fall was accidental."

I was moving through our main room, the others trailing. Phillips still carried the stone cat. "This thing hurled itself almost on my head. I came out of my room when I heard the noise—I thought somebody was trying to knock me out."

I wasn't interested then. I put Lita down on the bed just as Carol came in. "The doctor will be right over. I'm so sorry, Paul." I grunted an acceptance of her sympathy. "Wring a wash cloth out in cool water and bring it here, Carol." I felt sick—sicker than I had ever felt in my life. If anything happened to Lita—everything was over for me.

Her eyes opened. They lighted up briefly. "Paul," she murmured, and the lids dropped back. I bent over her, but before I could even speak, she was unconscious again. I heard Clancy say, "Get back to your room, Phillips, and stay there. Here, give me that thing you got."

He came over to the bed as Carol came with the washrag. "You don't think she's hurt bad?"

I sponged her brow. "I don't know, Clancy."

"Her color's good. It's lucky I was on tonight—I'll be watching that fellow and the rest of them. The Inspector was short of men. It was the least I could do." He didn't ask what we were doing prowling around the house at night, probably hiding evidence—at least up to no good.

The doctor came and Carol followed Clancy into the main room. He made a quick and efficient examination after I explained that she had fallen down the steps. Lita opened her eyes. Her arms came up to me in that appealing gesture. She wasn't aware of the doctor and neither was I.

He coughed. I explained to Lita, "You fell down the steps. The doctor is here." Her eyes clouded as she remembered back to her emotion. "Don't worry, honey. I'll explain later," I told her.

Finally he said, "A broken vertebrosternal." We stared at

him in such consternation that he laughed. "Cracked rib. You're a very lucky girl—falls can be serious things. At your age healing will be swift."

He worked swiftly taping Lita up, "You have a few bruises. And you will probably be downright sore for a few days. Take aspirin, stay in bed and don't worry." Like doctors the world over he went cheerfully on his way after telling us to do the impossible. Don't worry! How could we help worrying with one murder already consummated and no doubt others contemplated?

Because I knew as I kissed Lita that she had been meant to die. The attic steps are hard enough to negotiate at any time. A hazard on them made them lethal. I shivered at the memory of Phillips advancing with the stone cat. What he said might be true and again it might not.

"Honey, you didn't think I was in the attic with Carol because I wanted to be there?"

She was so weak and shaken that tears filled her eyes. "But why were you, Paul?"

"She wanted to get some letters she had dreamed about. I couldn't let her go up alone. I hated it, Lita, leaving you alone."

"When I saw her in my best negligee—the one I only wear for you, Paul—"

"I know, honey. We shouldn't talk about it now. You know I love you. Does anything else matter?" I did my best to prove it to her.

"You have to sleep now, Lita—it's Sunday morning."

I wanted to give her some aspirin, but Brundage still had the bottle. "I know something that always puts you to sleep." I read to her from "Electro High Frequency Technique." That had worked before when she had insisted on being a real partner and making me read aloud from my books. Imagine a dancer wanting to know such things!

I fell asleep almost before she did.

George and Carol woke me up two hours later. They had the morning papers. Mrs. Selton had made the front page. It was uncanny—reading of her heinous and sudden death and then looking into the eyes of the picture that accompanied the text. Because it was just like looking into Carol's eyes, right beside us. The picture had been taken at the time of her marriage, before the goitre had pushed the eyes forward. The hair was different but the features were the same as Carol's.

Lita was still asleep—I had closed the bedroom door. George apologized for not waking up. He was very sorry about Lita. I told them what the doctor had said—not too much harm done.

Mr. Selton's picture was also in the papers. The Seltons were an old family—what happened to them was news. I kept returning to the pictures. He had been wealthy, a society man with an assured position—member of the best clubs. What had sent him in the direction of Carrie O'Toole? She had undoubtedly been beautiful, but even after all these years she often lapsed into the expressions of South Boston. She told her cards every day.

Had he been trying to escape from something, some stuffiness perhaps that Carrie antidoted, or that he thought she would? Had the marriage been successful?

There was a knock on the door. Brundage and Lovelace fluttered on the threshold. They were both in black with white ruching about the neck and sleeves—a depressing pair in more ways than one. "We have not slept a wink all night," Brundage exclaimed.

"Come in." What else could I do except to hint that Brundage pitch her voice below its high querulousness? "Lita is asleep."

"How can she sleep? I thought we would all be murdered in our beds. I shivered so that my bed shook. I thought they were in with poor Evelyn. I finally called and she told me the door was locked and bolted—that we had nothing to fear." Characteristically she had not lowered her voice. "When I think of how comfortable things used to be."

I had got them seated in their stiff mourning finery, on the love seat. Something psychological in their affinity for love seats. They jumped when I said, "I think there was murderous intention last night. Somebody placed the stone cat on the attic stairway so that Lita would tumble and break her neck."

Brundage exclaimed, "And did she?"

"No, but it was pure accident that she didn't. George says that two of the thin balusters are broken off where the stone image fell through when her feet struck it. She would have noticed it on the way up, had it been there. You may not have noticed, but the attic stairs are steep and narrow."

Lovelace inquired, "What was she doing in the attic?"

I answered tiredly, "That's a long story."

Carol took over. "You might as well know. We didn't do anything wrong." Her tone was belligerent. "After what you said that my grandmother called me, Miss Brundage, I had to prove it wasn't true. My mother and father were married and right away! I have the letter to prove it." She held her hand out to George. "Give me the letters, George."

The old gals stared avidly when George handed over the beribboned packet. Carol was anxious to satisfy their curiosity. "I knew the letters were up there in Grandma's trunk. Mother told me she had written and never received an answer. Then, last night—" a mystic look came over her face— "Mother came to me. I saw her just as plain as I see you now. I thought it was just a nightmare at first . . ." At this point I went over and picked our key from the carpet, tangible evidence that somebody knew how to get in locked doors. I remarked casually, "We shall have a bolt, too, tomorrow morning at daybreak."

Brundage gave a demonstration of her best shivering. "You mean somebody did come in last night. Why?"

Before I could think up a good answer Carol said stubbornly, "It was my mother. If it wasn't, why was the attic door open and the trunk open too? It took me only a minute to get the letters—they were right on top waiting for me."

"Get on with the letter, Carol." Her stubborn mysticism was hard to swallow.

She began to read, "Dearest Mother, This is to apprise you of my marriage to Raoul. The wedding took place at the parsonage of the Rev. Peter Endicott at Providence, Rhode Island. For your benefit I am sending the train stubs. You will notice they are for different trains. Raoul, impeccable as always in his conduct, thought it best that I go directly to the minister's home and be in his charge until he could join me later in the morning. Rev. and Mrs. Endicott were wonderful to me. They did not mind the unseemly hour at which I arrived. They have promised to send you the notice when it appears in the Providence papers. They will also be happy to answer any questions that come to your mind.

"I am sorry it had to be this way. I did want you to be with us, Mother, but you would never let me bring Raoul to the house. But I am glad that we are going to live in Virginia away from everything that might spoil our happiness. I am so happy. I know that I could never be this happy in Cambridge. I want to live my own life and have my husband all to myself. I can not share him with anyone. He has to be mine!

"Raoul joins me in extending you the hospitality of our home. Please write and say that I did right. I never wanted to cause you any sorrow. Your loving daughter, Evie."

There was something poignant about the letter. I could understand the break in Carol's voice as she ended. There was fierce independence and yet a pleading dependence that the daughter probably didn't understand herself. Her insistence on not sharing the husband—a fierce possessiveness that was almost morbid. Was she afraid that her mother would interfere?

Lovelace said, "That is a very touching letter, my dear. It throws new light on Evie and her mother."

Brundage snorted, "Well! Carrie certainly kept her news to herself. She told us time and again that she had never heard one word from Evie after she sneaked out of this house in the middle of the night with that man."

"He wasn't 'that man.' He was my father and a very fine man. He took the most wonderful care of Mother. He wouldn't go any place without her. After she died he didn't care to live. He still had me and he was always kind, but it was Mother that he loved with all his heart. That last year when she was sick, she talked so much about this house and about Grandma—she never had much before."

Carol, who had been so sad, suddenly smiled. "He used to try to make her laugh. He said it was an old castle haunted by a witch. And that she was the beautiful princess he had rescued from the witch, so they could be happy forever after."

"I must say!" Brundage breathed indignation. "That was hardly a suitable word for his mother-in-law! No wonder you have no manners."

"He might not have meant it, Amy," Lovelace offered. "He was from the South, you know, and that might have been part of his folklore. I saw him once when he came right up to the front door and boldly announced that he had come to see Miss Evie. The maid was having trouble with him, so I dismissed him."

"Why couldn't he call on Mother?" Carol demanded.

"My dear! She had met him on Indian Wharf. Evie had gone there with her easel against her mother's express desires. She should not have spoken to him. It was unsuitable in every way."

"I wish I could have known my father then. Was he handsome?"

"Yes, you might have termed him handsome. His hair curled and it was quite long. The boldness of his eyes was a detraction. And his clothing was hardly appropriate for a late afternoon call. It made it impossible to ask him in for tea."

Lita called then and I hurried into the bedroom. She looked so much better. I propped her up in bed and brought the papers to her. "We're famous, honey. Our domicile has even made the *Boston Globe*." She smiled wanly. I opened the windows wider to the lovely June day. "We have company, darling. Even the dear old ladies next door are in. They seem to be less afraid of us than they are of Phillips and Oglesbie. After due consideration, and the coming of morning, perhaps even Brundage finds it difficult to regard us as murderers."

"Don't, Paul."

"Okay, honey. I'll sneak in some coffee and rolls and fruit juice."

Barely finished with this agreeable chore when Dr. Oglesbie was at the door. He knocked and had to be admitted with whatever grace I could muster. The old ladies tucked in their feet, remembering his skeletal approach. It was strange that in our confusion and suspicion of each other, we were nevertheless inclined to seek company.

Oglesbie explained that Phillips was making it impossible for him to concentrate. "He is re-enacting the murder—taking all roles. He screams like a strangled female one minute and growls hatred the next. The funny thing, though—" he moistened his red lips and looked at each of us to make sure we would enjoy the humor— "he keeps talking as though she were hanged. 'Strung up like a beef, swaying in the damp dungeon'—a weird performance!"

We none of us found any humor to smile at. I said lamely, "Probably a snatch of a song," but I was sorry immediately. It didn't help.

I tried another tack. "It's strange, Doctor, that you did not make an appearance last night. Didn't you hear anything?"

He smiled enigmatically. "I heard a great deal." His small eyes held a concentrated malice as they rested on

Carol. He watched her hand the letters to George. "But since I seem to be under grave suspicion in this house—since the smallest act on my part is construed as salacious and diabolical—I thought it more expedient to remain in my room."

"Haven't you any curiosity?"

"Not in the usual sense of the word. I have scientific curiosity . . ." His eyes remained glued to the packet of letters. I wondered if he knew a great deal more than he pretended. It might have been he who had been in the attic. Carol always said that he exercised a peculiar influence over her grandmother. He might have been looking for some papers in her trunk—have moved the letters to get at something else. Putting the stone cat in Lita's downward path was more characteristic of his small nature than of the sea-faring Phillips.

He hadn't once asked what the noise was about. Perhaps he knew. At any rate, while he regaled his unwilling listeners with a complete survey of his large and scientific mind, I got up and with my back to Oglesbie told Carol that I would put the letters in the drawer for safe-keeping. They might not be of interest to Oglesbie, but knowing how Carol valued them, I did not want them to fall into his hands. It might have been he who was in our rooms last night. With a sheet around him, he could easily play ghost. In our present state of mind, we would hardly challenge even a "ghost." I remember how unreasonably frightened I had been during the night.

I tossed the letters into the highboy drawer, hoping that I hadn't been observed. As they landed upside-down, I saw that the bottom letter was addressed to Miss Evelyn Lovelace. I smiled in spite of myself. Carrie and her eccentricities! If Lovelace knew that Carrie had filched even her letters, she would undoubtedly be furious. People didn't do common things of that sort to the Lovelaces, formerly of Beacon Hill.

Then I noticed something that surprised me. Lita had said it was gone. Had Mrs. Selton taken it, accidentally broken it, and then seen fit to toss it back in the drawer? No, because when Lita mentioned it—Mrs. Selton was already dead. She couldn't have returned it.

But it was back in the drawer—the ragged edges of the ancient ivory mute evidence that it had been snapped in two. Only the upper part of the backscratcher was there—the claw-like hand was gone.

CHAPTER EIGHT

As I TURNED back to these people in the house I was struck
by the fact that I knew very little about them. You can live
in the same house with people through a winter and part
of a spring—you think you understand all their little
quirks and idiosyncrasies, but a crisis can come up and
you realize they are all strangers to you—as though you
had met them while out walking.

Sunday mornings when we were awake, we had always
seen the old ladies, including Mrs. Selton at times, going
fussily to church, breathing sanctimoniousness designed
to put us to shame. But there they sat, excepting Mrs.
Selton, who was on a slab at the morgue, as though they
intended to sit there through the week.

I opened the door into the bedroom, after giving Lita
the wherewithal to wash and comb and bed-jacket herself—

Dr. Oglesbie hadn't yet inquired as to her indisposition—so that she could see and hear our guests, painful as it might be.

I had to entertain them. "Miss Lovelace, I was interested in Mrs. Selton's picture in the morning papers—she was very beautiful."

"She was." Her voice was dry and strained as though it were difficult to think back that far. "She had great beauty."

"I'm not so sure of that," Brundage said. "She was pretty in a common sort of way—like a wild flower."

Lovelace squelched her. "She was the most beautiful woman I have ever known. I should know—I saw enough of her."

The room was quiet. Church bells sounded through historic Cambridge while the heat built up on the heavy stiff furnishings and Miss Lovelace held her hands tightly together and began to tell the story of Carrie O'Hoole.

"I could understand, when it seemed nobody else in Boston could, Thomas Selton's infatuation with her." She looked defiantly around at us to crush our possible disbelief. "Her hair was like spun gold. It curled around her face even when she piled it high on her head. Thomas liked it down in a cloud covering her shoulders—it fell below her waist."

Brundage cut in spitefully, "She had to cut it, though, before Evie was born, and when she heard that long hair sapped one's strength she kept it cut. Not bobbed, of course—no decent woman would wear her hair like a man's—but just short enough to turn under."

Lovelace silenced her with a well bred look. "She had brown eyes, very large, and fine features. Which was remarkable, because her parents were not gifted with exceptional looks."

Brundage laughed, "They were the commonest of common stock. Why, the mother took in washing and the father was a hod carrier or something. I wish you would not talk in such a hushed tone, Evelyn. You know that Carrie was a hat check girl at the Parker House when Thomas met her. I'll admit she was pretty, but it didn't last long. She faded faster than any girl I ever saw. That's the trouble with blondes. You wouldn't have noticed her, Evelyn, if Thomas Selton hadn't got entangled with her."

"That is quite true. I would never have met her. I would have seen her probably as others did, but . . ."

"She simply would have been below your notice. How Thomas Selton—why, hundreds of men saw her every day, but they knew their position in the world. He discovered to his sorrow that beauty is only skin deep."

"If you will let me proceed, Amy. When I returned from a tour of the continent, Thomas called on me. I was happy to see him because we were old friends . . ."

Amy glanced at her quickly. "Why, everybody thought you were engaged. We thought your party was to announce that engagement. I remember how excited I was."

Evelyn pinched her lips together. Amy's prattling usually annoyed her. "My party was a home-coming one—

to welcome my friends back to our house. As I tried to say, Thomas told me he had received the invitation and in the next breath he asked me to include Carrie O'Toole.

"Naturally I was stunned at first. I did not know the girl. I had never heard of her. I did not believe he was genuinely interested in her—when he told me of her background. She had no education to speak of . . ."

"I doubt if she went beyond the third grade," from Brundage.

Carol reminded her, "You seem to forget in your spitefulness that Grandmother is dead."

"The truth's the truth, at any time. And if you want the truth, I don't believe that your grandmother ever liked me. She was often very rude. I did not live in this house to be with her, but to be with my best friend, Miss Lovelace."

"My mother," continued Lovelace, "was stunned when I put my request before her, but I reminded her that her position was secure—she could do whatever she wished— and that I thought it would be a very fine thing for Thomas to see this girl among the people with whom he intended to place her."

Amy laughed, a thin brittle tinkle. "She came, she was seen, but she didn't conquer. I never in my life saw a girl so out of place. Her flaming beauty was an insult to the other girls. And her dress—her mother must have made it between trips to the clothesline!"

Carol said, "She conquered Grandfather. That was what counted. I'm proud of her!"

Evelyn looked at her but said nothing. Finally, as though talking to herself, she went on, "She laughed a great deal that night. I could hear her laughter wherever I turned."

"No wonder," Brundage added, "it was so loud. She had no idea at first that she was a misfit. You would have thought she was on a hayride party—so boisterous!"

Lovelace said, "Thomas came to me. He was worried. He wondered if they would ever accept her. He winced as her laughter came up to us, high and clear above the subdued murmur. I told him that I would continue to do my best for her. She was drinking too much champagne . . ."

Brundage chuckled, "She told me years later she thought it was cider."

"He didn't commit himself when I said, 'If you are sure you love her . . .' However, I went to the most important personage at the party, Mrs. Lancaster Bettle, and asked if I could present Carrie O'Toole. Mrs. Bettle was one of my godmothers," she ignored Amy's spiteful chuckling, "and usually indulgent to me, but she was very hard of hearing. She kept shouting, 'Who is she, Evelyn? The O'Tooles, who are they? There are no O'Tooles in Boston.'"

Amy couldn't contain herself longer. "That was so amusing, considering their number in sections of Boston. Everybody stopped to listen and to smile. You remember how Thomas looked when he swept Carrie over in front of Mrs. Bettle?"

Evidently Evelyn did. Because her face tightened at the

memory. She let Brundage carry on while her mind stayed with the distressing picture. "She shouted at Thomas, 'Is this the one? Stand up, girl, and quit trembling. I never bit anybody in my life.' She raised her lorgnette and stared at poor Carrie. You could trust Mrs. Bettle to know everybody that was worth knowing in Boston, and she knew that Carrie didn't belong.

"Poor Carrie! I am afraid she had had too much champagne. She stood there with her mouth open and let the champagne from her glass dribble over Mrs. Bettle's gown."

"Don't be unkind, Amy."

"I am not being unkind. I am telling the truth. It was a scene I shall never forget. Mrs. Bettle screamed, 'You little fool. Take her away, Thomas. She's gauche.' And Thomas, his face black with anger, said, 'You old battlewagon! You've been launched finally. See if you can do one kind act before you sink into Davey Jones' Locker.' He turned around to the assembled guests and he said, 'It gives me great pleasure to introduce to you my future wife, Miss Carrie O'Toole.' "

"Good for Grandfather!" Carol shouted.

Brundage said, "Yes, he made his bed and he lay down in it, to quote a vulgar expression, but to the day of his death I could not understand it."

"Wasn't he happy, Miss Lovelace?" Carol appealed to her.

Miss Lovelace turned to look at the young girl as though she found the question startling. "He never said."

"Of course he wasn't happy," Brundage insisted. "I never could understand why he went through with the marriage. I thought he would settle a sum of money on her, as gentlemen did."

Carol said, "You have a filthy mind, Miss Brundage."

Dr. Oglesbie spoke up, "You are ignorant of the mores of a cultured society, Miss Caroline. The higher the society the more rigid the rules."

"Hush your face!" she said disrespectfully.

I didn't blame her; after all, it was her grandmother that Brundage was picking to pieces. And Oglesbie was too stuffy to countenance. Still, I was anxious to hear this background. I couldn't help but feel that it would throw some light on Mrs. Selton's unhappiness and maybe the murder. I picked up the thread of the conversation. "I suppose everybody who counted expected him to marry Miss Lovelace rather than Miss O'Toole?"

"Might I request that you keep my name out of this?"

"What he says is true, Evelyn. You may have refused Thomas Selton at one time, as you said, but I always felt that you expected him to renew his court. You know, we never thought it quite ladylike to accept the first offer —Miss Fairley always insisted that we not capitulate too soon."

George surprisingly tossed a barb. "You mean to say that you got a first offer from someone, Miss Brundage?"

She bridled. "I could have had many offers if I had conducted myself the way young ladies do nowadays." She stared at the length of leg Carol had exposed. It was significant enough to make Carol bring her legs discreetly under her and attempt to cover her knees. She shot a look of hatred at Oglesbie rather than at Brundage.

I tried again. "So the wedding came off in proper time?"

"It occurred, if that is what you mean," Lovelace replied loftily. "Beacon Hill would not accept Carrie, so Thomas bought this Walsh place."

"I never, never could understand it, Evelyn. You stuck by Carrie through all her snubs, and you made a superhuman effort to get your friends to accept her. It wouldn't have been so hard on you if she had been grateful, but she wasn't."

"Maybe she wanted to live her own life, as Mother said she wanted to in her letter?"

"Her own life?" Brundage questioned. "How could she? She had married Thomas Selton. His mother was dead. She was the female head of the house. There were charities, church bazaars, ladies' committee meetings, all sorts of fine human projects that the Selton women had always contributed to."

"Send them a check and let them manage. If they didn't want her, why should she give them her time?" Carol reasoned.

"You are a fine example of heredity, my dear. That was exactly what your grandmother wanted to do, but a Selton of Boston can not do that. It was her presence that was demanded as well as her husband's money. If it had not been for Evelyn representing the family, there would have been no place saved for Evie."

"For Mother?" Carol asked.

"Yes, for your mother," Brundage snapped. "Of course, Evelyn couldn't have known that the sacrifice would be in vain. She gave the best years of her life—in fact all her life—to help your family, and I must say the end did not justify the sacrifice." This wasn't very flattering as she looked at Carol.

"Please, Amy! One can't always foresee and perhaps it is just as well. I can only say that I did my duty as I saw it. Thomas pleaded with me always to help Carrie adjust herself to society."

Brundage was in again with the acid remembrances. "All Carrie wanted to do was to visit that family of hers and just exist like an animal." She shushed Carol's attempted interruption. "Why, even you would not have enjoyed seeing your great-grandmother, with her coarse red hands, and common speech. And your grandmother wanted to be married in that parlor with its cheap fringes and plaster saints. Thomas had sense enough to put his foot down. Evelyn had the wedding in her home."

"So my grandmother couldn't even have her wedding the way she wanted. Did you go on the honeymoon with them, Miss Lovelace?"

Brundage gasped at this insult to her friend and tears filled Miss Lovelace's eyes. Carol apologized, "I'm sorry,

Miss Lovelace. You probably did what you thought proper. But you don't know what it is to want to do things your own way."

"I think I do, my dear, but doesn't that depend on how improper it is? Carrie's parlor was not suitable. Even she saw that later. I especially invited her parents, although Thomas was not in favor of it. He knew that people would make capital of it. But after all, they were her parents, as I pointed out."

I could just imagine the poor, perspiring parents of Carrie. So could Carol, if her ingenuous face was any proof.

"You were beautiful at the wedding, Evelyn. You had sent to Paris especially for your gown. I thought it was a lovely gesture. There were so many compliments for you that poor Carrie was quite piqued."

"I had offered to pick out her gown but she would not let me. Of course she didn't know the right dressmakers— some woman in South Boston sewed it up."

"'Sewed it up' was correct. But her lack of poise was the determining factor. Even Thomas became annoyed."

Carol had dogged determination. "What happened after their marriage?"

Lovelace said, "That was a brilliant winter in Boston. There were so many parties that the round of gayety was almost tiring. We had a Russian grand duke staying with us."

"Why didn't you marry him, Evelyn? I often wondered. He was so handsome."

"I never cared for Russia," Evelyn replied blandly.

"Well, I think you should have instead of devoting your life to Carrie Selton. You were a saint, everybody said so. It was a losing battle—your trying to pry a niche loose for Carrie. She tried hard but she could not succeed. She caused you no end of embarrassment—you remember that time at Mrs. Jack Gardner's?"

"I'm dying to hear that," George said.

Brundage took this to mean enthusiasm. "Evelyn took her there to an evening reception. I had a wonderful time that night. Evelyn had selected a gown for Carrie. It was a beautiful creation, moulded to the figure with yards and yards at the hem." She stopped to enjoy a laugh. "But even then Carrie could not carry it off. She did not know how to walk. Evelyn and I had had several years at Miss Fairley's where proper walking was emphasized. Carrie wrapped herself in that gown like a mummy. She could not move. Not even when Mrs. Gardner, at Evelyn's behest, asked her to come and sit by her. Naturally everyone was much amused."

"You know what I think, Miss Brundage? I think you were so jealous of Grandma that you would gladly have . . ." Fortunately George clamped a hand over her mouth before she accused Miss Brundage of the murder.

CHAPTER NINE

THE ROOM WAS very still. Brundage's small eyes couldn't hold the hate she had nursed for years. It spilled over on her wrinkled visage and poured onto Carol, whose eyes were wide with fright. She evidently hadn't meant to say what she did. It shocked her. George withdrew his hand and she touched her lips with her finger while she continued to stare back at Brundage, whose small hands were working in a fury of resentment.

I cleared my throat with an effort. The atmosphere was heavy with heat and hate, suspicion and dread. My words sounded hollow—made to order. "After all, Mrs. Selton had a happy life in this fine old home, didn't she, Miss Lovelace?"

"She should have. Thomas was generous. I engaged the servants myself. Carrie had not the slightest idea how to proceed or how to conduct herself with them. Often I had to discharge them and search the town for others who knew their place."

Brundage chuckled. She hadn't dropped her hate, merely redirected it. "Servants were her best friends! Thomas would come home to find her stirring an Irish stew while the cook rocked in comfort. She dressed her own maid's hair!"

"Don't be harsh, Amy. She didn't realize."

"She got cranky enough as she got older. I never saw anybody get more work out of a woman than she did out of old Annie."

Carol asked, "When did Grandmother develop the goitre?"

"Before your mother was born," Lovelace replied. "Thomas was so distressed. He spoke to the best surgeons. He even offered to take her to Vienna to have it cut out, but she had a dread . . ."

"And why shouldn't she? You remember that woman, Evelyn, that woman who had her goitre removed?" At Evelyn's blank stare, her temper broke. "There are times, Evelyn, when you show your age! You don't remember things any more."

"I remember the important things." Which should have snubbed Brundage but didn't. The sour one grabbed the story thread. "She lived in Uphams Corner. I remember it just as though it were yesterday." She surveyed us proudly, then turned to refresh Lovelace's memory. "She was one of your charity patients. You told me about her and told me not to tell Carrie. But I was not going to let Carrie go through the same experience. I got the address from you and took her out there, so that she could see what Thomas was driving her to."

She described the woman. "She looked terrible, not even human. Her eyes darted out at us. She was nothing but skin and bones. Her mother showed us a picture of her before the operation—she was plump and pretty. But she would not let her mother near her. She clung to the sides of the bed and screamed that the bed was being tipped, that her mother was trying to throw her out on the floor. She was like a wild animal, all claws and wild eyes.

"That settled things for Carrie. She refused to have an operation. You heard her, Evelyn, thank me again and again.'"

I spoke sharply. "You shouldn't have interfered. That wouldn't have happened to Mrs. Selton. She would have had expert care. The woman you mention had her parathyroid removed along with the thyroid. It sometimes happens with bungling surgery."

"I don't think you know anything about it. I know what I saw with my own eyes and I wasn't going to have Carrie lose her mind and her looks."

Carol's voice was deadly. "You were very sweet to Grandmother, weren't you? What good were her looks with that horrible growth on her neck? Or her mind either, with all of you beating at her?" Her lips trembled.

"I can imagine how she felt. Having that thing growing on her and afraid to have anything done."

"It did change her," Lovelace said kindly. "I tried to make her enthusiastic about Vienna and the gay life there. I offered to take care of Evie and the house during her absence, but she just sat and stared in front of her."

"What did Grandfather do? After the goitre became large?"

"Do? Why, he went on as usual. He had a great many duties. His business to look after. His properties. I helped both of them in every way I could."

"Did Grandfather—did he still love her?"

Lovelace showed her surprise at the question. "He never said, my dear. In those days marriage was a sacred institution and Thomas Selton was an honorable man."

This didn't satisfy Carol. "But you saw so much of them—together. Do you think he was ever sorry?"

As though she were thinking of sacred marriage and all that it implied, Lovelace's face lighted up like a young girl's at her first love affair. "Naturally he never discussed it." Her lips firmed but the light stayed in her eyes. "He had got what he wanted. Why should he be sorry?"

"Phth!" Brundage exploded. "He was sorry till the day he died. I don't know how it could have escaped your attention, Evelyn. He was ashamed to have her sit at the head of his table. You did that, Evelyn. And presided at receptions."

"Not really?" Carol gasped.

"Amy is exaggerating as usual. I presided in Carrie's place at her insistence. Thomas had social obligations. He sat at the head of his table. I merely represented Carrie, carefully explaining to the guests that she was ill."

"They probably thought she was of unsound mind and had to be kept in her room!" Carol voiced her indignation. "I think it was unforgivable. With your breeding, Miss Lovelace, I am surprised you accepted the situation."

Lovelace sat up straight. Her eyes hardened. Brundage replied for her, "If you had breeding you wouldn't question her actions. It wasn't easy for her. Many times I found her in tears. Especially after that evening when a guest addressed her as Mrs. Selton . . ."

"Amy!" The memory was still painful for Miss Lovelace. Color seeped up into her white face, brightening the patrician features.

"I'm telling only the truth. Your migraine attacks started then. And you had never been ill a day in your life before. And precious little thanks you got for your sacrifice. Evie was the hardest child to rear that I ever heard of!"

"Don't tell me you did that too?" Carol was close to insolence.

Lovelace's head turned slowly in her direction. "It was impossible to evade. Your grandmother had no contact with anybody who counted. It was unthinkable that Thomas' child should be neglected."

Brundage said, "She had none of Thomas' traits and she didn't have her mother's looks. I have seen her scream until her face was black. I used to long to inflict corporal punishment myself. I never could understand it. She had the best governesses that money could buy, yet they would not keep her at Miss Buxton's school. They said she was common." Brundage said it proudly as a farmer will when he displays a two-headed calf.

Carol spoke through stiff lips, successfully holding back the tears. "Mother never spoke of her youth. I used to wonder what it was like up North and I would ask her. All she ever told me about was the snow—how it looked like white frosting on a cake you weren't allowed to touch. Daddy told me once that Mother had never been happy as a child and that I mustn't ask her about it."

"If she wasn't happy, it was her own fault!" Brundage glared at Carol. "Even Thomas could do nothing with her. She would close her mouth like a clam and stare boldly at him. She never even acted like a lady until he died. The shock of seeing him dead in his chair with his eyes open—he had a stroke—"

"Amy!" Miss Lovelace found Brundage's details too morbid. "You are showing poor taste."

"Well, I am telling the truth." Her usual excuse. "I will say this much. Evie did apologize to you for her actions. His death awakened her to her position in the world. She asked you to come to the house to live and to introduce her to society."

"Yes," Lovelace mused, "I had to remind her that that was hardly the time to think of society. That we must all go into mourning to do her father honor. Perhaps later . . ."

"Who would have thought that in less than ten years she would elope, never to be seen again . . ."

"Why didn't you help her, Miss Lovelace?" Carol spoke quietly as you do to a maiden aunt who is slightly deaf. "It seems to me it would have been so easy. Mother was always so reasonable and never one to run away."

Lovelace sighed, "I had her mother to take care of. As was to be expected of one of Carrie's temperament, she became hysterical. Evie was shocked at some of the accusations she hurled, even at me. Evie became sullen. When I had succeeded in making your grandmother see reason, Evie wouldn't talk to me. She took her small talent and went to Haymarket, Scollay Square and the wharves. The daubs she made were an insult to art and to fine sensibilities. Her mother agreed that they be destroyed."

"Oh! I think that was criminal!"

Brundage agreed with Carol, "You are right. I saw one myself of a—a prostitute! No nice girl would even have looked at that creature, her clothes half torn off, lying there intoxicated, one limb . . ."

"Amy!" Amy had enough blood to blush at the peremptory command from Lovelace.

"What I mean—it was criminal to destroy Mother's work. She did right to run away—she couldn't win, not here. If I had only known!" Carol was unable to control her tears. She let them run down her face unnoticed. "If

I had only known about Grandmother too! Sometimes I almost hated her when she said those things about Mother. Why did she, though? Why did she—when she had these letters?"

Her impassioned plea to us went unanswered. There was a sharp knock at the door. Brundage whispered shrilly, "Don't answer. It's that Phillips. Don't let him in."

The door was pounded. "Open up!"

I walked over and opened the door. One of the homicide squad who had been there the night before sent his sleep-heavy eyes from me to the circle of frightened faces. "The chief wants to see you downstairs."

"Me?" forgetting my grammar.

"Yes. And the rest of the gang." On his own he was quite a tough-sounding lad. "Just file out—all of you—and don't do anything funny. He's receivin' in the droring-room."

Lovelace didn't appreciate his humor. "This is the Sabbath, young man. I don't care to see your chief today."

"Yeah? Well, you'll see him and like it. And don't remind him what day it is or he'll get sore and think he ought to be home. He grows petunias—under glass." He gave us this information with a wicked gleam in his heavy eyes, as though the Inspector liked to cut his children's nails to the quick.

Dr. Oglesbie, who had risen and was wiping his soft hands, reprimanded him, "Officer, watch your language. We will be glad to accompany you to the drawing-room if the Inspector insists, but refrain from insulting these ladies or answer for the consequences."

"Okay, bud, you win. But only because you're so damn funny. Get going!"

The ladies walked out with much rustling of ancient taffeta while I explained to the officer about Lita. He walked past me into the bedroom and surveyed Lita. The survey was too appreciative. But his glance at me was not. "Go on down. He can come up to see the lady."

I reassured Lita and followed the others. But not before I saw that the detective intended joining me. He stayed a step behind me.

I forgot him when I saw Inspector Green seated before the marble-topped table. It was all right for him to sit down. That didn't bother me. It was problematical whether he had slept since the murder. But his face was grave and he was waiting for me. His eyes reached up to impale me the way you pierce a hot dog with a fork.

I didn't know that I was standing still halfway down the stairs. All I saw was the object that lay on its bit of tissue in front of the Inspector. I had seen it before. It had something to do with the murder—something significant.

But what? Mrs. Selton had been strangled with her silken scarf. There had been a paper with the words, "The Stroke of Death." Did they actually mean something? Was that thing—that suddenly gruesome object part of some death design?

There was a prod in my floating ribs. "You scared? Quit stalling."

I resumed our march. There were butterflies in the pit of my stomach. I was scared. I wanted to go back up and talk to Lita. The way we used to do about the home we were going to have. It wasn't much—just a small white house, with fir trees singing at night . . . soughing, the way they do on the West coast when only they can feel the wind. There was a picket fence and flowers . . . Lita wasn't standing among the flowers. She was nowhere around. I listened for her laughter . . . there was only the gruff voice in my ear, "Christ, man, have you got palsy?"

They had made room for me. I stood in front of it. The jagged end where it had been snapped off. The cunning fingers curled for stroking, delicately daubed with a repulsive substance. I could hear Lita saying it . . . Even then it had sounded artificial . . . or had it? "It's gone, Paul." How would she know it had gone unless . . .

I swore at myself. What the hell was I trying to do?

The Inspector was smiling at me—that cynical way that might have been good for petunias under glass but was poison for me. "I see that you intend making my work easy. I am grateful. You have seen this object before. You can hardly take your eyes from it. It fascinates you. You pushed it down the throat of Mrs. Selton . . ."

"And what was she doing all that time . . . calmly letting me go ahead without protest?"

"I'm waiting for you to tell me."

"I wasn't there at the time."

His widening smile creased his face, "So you admit that you came down after your wife finished the job. I thought this was a feminine job—it has those delicate touches so dear to the heart of women."

I stared back at him, my heart pounding like a crazy thing. I could feel the others drawing away from me, Brundage making noises like a hound closing in on the rabbit—glad little yelps. That curiosity about people in dramatic moments that I'm seldom able to suppress made me turn to these people of the house. Lovelace looked sorrowful and without malice. Brundage looked the way I knew she would, only more so. Phillips was going up the stairs—he had been questioned ahead of us. George dropped his eyes before mine and turned to examine a Corot landscape that didn't remind him of South Dakota. Carol stared past me, her nose elevated, her eyes stiff. I could sense no change in Oglesbie—he might have been listening to something on the radio.

The Inspector coveted my attention. "Mr. Redfern!" I was glad for the mister. "What is this object?" He pointed to the gruesome piece of evidence.

"I thought you knew. It's a back scratcher."

"It belongs to you?"

"Yes."

"How did you acquire it?"

"It was given to us."

He smiled at my admission of the "us."

"How long has it been in your possession?"

"I don't know. Six months . . . maybe longer."

"You had it in your rooms until last night?"

"So far as I know it was there until shortly before the murder. I don't have time to take inventory every night."

"But you did take inventory of this object at least and found it conveniently gone just before the murder. Did you confide this loss to anyone—in such a way that you would have an alibi for not having it in your possession?"

"I'm afraid I didn't think of that."

He gave a bastard chuckle and got up. "Maybe your wife can elaborate."

He must have seen the pain in my eyes. His face dropped the false smile. I watched him fold the tissue about the ivory hand. He held it carefully so as not to spoil the dried mucus. I thought of Lita and my heart did a flip-flop. I dogged his steps but he closed the door carefully almost on my nose.

The ivory hand had come back, trailing its slime of murder.

CHAPTER TEN

WHAT WOULD LITA say to him? Would he trap her into some terrible admission? He was clever—smooth as nylon and twice as strong. Pressing my ear hard against the door, I could hear a low mumble of voices—that was all. The back of my neck felt like a two by four that pressed against my shoulders. Sweat rolled down from it.

The air in the hall was sultry. I moved back and forth. Phillips was jabbering in his room, "Put your tongue back in your mouth! Don't swing there goggling at me! And you too put your tongue back in your mouth!" What a lot of company he seemed to have and what pleasant company.

Why the devil wasn't Inspector Green questioning him? He was by-passing him very neatly to concentrate on us. Any fool could see that Phillips would be more apt to strangle a woman than either of us. But the Inspector was clever. He knew that this was done by a woman! Damn him!

The two by four traveled down to take the place of my spine. I walked over and quietly opened the door. To our rooms. I hadn't made a sound—it had been as easy as that. But the smart Inspector might have heard me—it would be like him not to let on. I stood still. The butterflies were having a dance inside me as I moved over to the highboy. I stood still again. Then my arm went out slowly and the drawer opened. He hadn't got there first.

The jagged piece of ivory lay just where I had seen it last—hateful now with its delicate carving. It weighed a ton as I picked it up and slipped it in my trouser pocket.

What they were saying came to my ears then. The oily voice of the Inspector, "You may as well tell the whole story, Mrs. Redfern. Once we have a thread we keep pulling on it. And the pulling hurts."

Lita's indignant, "But I don't know any more!"

I could feel the blood pound in my ears. Pushing his face in wouldn't help us. There would be another in his place —not so polished. I went back the way I had come. My hand was on the knob when I heard Lita insist, "That back scratcher was in the highboy, in the right hand side. It was there . . ."

I stepped out and closed the door. My hand went to the piece of ivory as I stood out in the hall. My eyes raced the length of the carpet. If there were only a place where I could hide it. But a piece of moulding fastened down the edges. It was probably safer on me, anyway. He had searched me once—he wouldn't search me again.

I opened the door boldly and slammed it. Then I walked into the bedroom. The Inspector smiled up at me. "Couldn't stand it any longer?" He stood up. "I'll see you again, Mrs. Redfern. I think it will be a good idea if you stay in bed. The doctor tells me you had rather a nasty fall. Strange that Clancy forgot to say anything about it."

Lita became excited, "Don't blame Clancy, Inspector Green. We didn't know we weren't supposed to move about the house. We didn't do any harm. Honest!"

He bestowed one of his beneficent smiles on us and walked into the other room. I heard him open the high-boy drawer but I didn't turn. Our door closed.

He was gone. The ivory handle felt hot through the cotton lining of my pocket. "Hot goods!" Articles the police wanted and that you had to hide until you could dispose of them.

"I don't think that he believed me, Paul, about that back scratcher." Her face was very young—flushed, the eyes troubled. I bent down and kissed her on the soft, full lips.

"It isn't his business to believe anyone." I sat down on the bed. I was tired.

"Do you think that he really believes that we—that I—"

"How the hell do I know what he thinks?" It was spoken so harshly that the fear deepened in Lita's eyes. She drew back against the headboard. "Forgive me, Lita.

This whole business hasn't improved my disposition." I tried to smile. It must have been a sickly imitation of the Inspector's. It didn't reassure Lita.

"How about something to eat? I feel hollow. Will one of my hybrid sandwiches and a cup of coffee suit?"

"Anything, Paul."

I made the sandwiches and boiled the water for drip. Each minute I expected the door to be pounded. Then I thought of something. "I'm going down and ask the Inspector about that 'Stroke of Death' business. He should have had the handwriting analyzed by this time."

I went out before Lita could protest and down the stairs. The Inspector was just going out the door. I called to him. He waited outside on the porch. "Thought of something you wanted to tell me?"

I thought only of how good my fist would feel smashing into his smug face. "I thought of something you could tell me."

"I might."

"Who wrote the note that was found under the chair?"

"Don't you know?"

"No, I don't!"

He almost laughed in my face. "I'll play along. It was written by Mrs. Selton."

I stared back at him. "She wrote it herself? But why? Could she have put that thing down her throat? She was the one we thought of right away as having taken it. It would be possible, wouldn't it, for her to tie the scarf around her own throat?"

He looked as pleased as a child watching a fly trying to step off of flypaper. "I expected you to present that theory. It troubled me when you didn't."

I just looked at him. There was nothing else I could do. I walked back in the house and up to Lita. The water had almost boiled away. I poured it over the coffee and took the sandwiches in.

"You look sick, Paul. What did the Inspector say?"

"He said that Mrs. Selton wrote the note herself."

I winced when she said, "That sounds like suicide. Do you suppose she took her quarrel with Carol that seriously?"

"God knows! Let's not talk about it, honey. Eat your sandwich." I went out to pour the coffee. It was black as night.

"Where are the others? Carol and George ought to come in. I thought for a while there we were going to have all of them. Wasn't that terrible when Carol almost accused Brundage of the murder?"

"Yes."

"I could hear all of you holding your breaths. Do you think she could have done it, Paul?"

"Sure. I think they all did it—all but us."

She grinned back at me. "You know, Paul, it sounds a little like voodoo—that note and the ivory back scratcher. Mrs. Selton had such queer superstitions."

"Voodoo couldn't happen in New England. They've got

plenty of their own brand here." I yawned. "I wish to God we were out on the Charles now in a boat."

"Paul, why do you suppose Miss Lovelace did so much for the Seltons?"

"Loyalty, I suppose. She didn't get married, so she had to mess around in somebody's life. She looks like the sort who likes to bend down to help someone less fortunate. It gave her a glow. Made her feel useful."

"But why didn't she marry? She must have had chances. Brundage as good as said that she was in love with Thomas."

"Oh, Brundage wouldn't see a fly on her nose. Old ladies love to cook up romances. Brundage couldn't cook up anything for herself, so she does it for Evelyn, then she warms her hands in the glow. You find a great many New England spinsters of that vintage—the times just weren't propitious for easy marriage. Why, even today, look at all the girls who are angling for husbands. What would have happened to you if you hadn't found a soft guy like me?"

She threw the spread over my face. I untangled myself. "That's no fair. I can't wrestle with you because your ribs are cracked."

Our half-hearted attempts at levity didn't fool either one of us. For the first time since we had known each other we both felt self-conscious. There were things I wanted to ask Lita, but if she knew the answers I didn't want to hear them. How had her earring got under the chair?

Why had she spent so much time downstairs? She was lithe and active—she could make the steps down and back in two shakes. Did she know anything more about the damn ivory hand? Did the Inspector really have some evidence that would implicate Lita? Or was he just trying to scare hell out of me?

"How about a book? Not technical this time."

"I hope not. Read a mystery. There's a new one in the drawer. I put it there so Carol wouldn't grab it before we had a chance to read it . . . I wonder why Carol doesn't come up?"

I could have told her but I didn't. "She's probably giving interviews to the press—she'd love that. She'll come up soon enough when she needs something."

"Don't be like that, Paul. It doesn't sound like you."

"Well, Carol has the makings of a first-class female heel if you ask me. But don't ask me." I had pulled out the drawer. It was the sight of the letters coupled with Carol's recent snootiness that angered me. "What in God's name do we want to read a mystery for when we've got a perfectly good one on our hands and probably on our heads?"

I slammed the drawer and picked up "War and Peace." I opened it at random and sprawled out in the chair by the bed. The Christmas maskers and the troika ride were remote enough from that Boston house of death on a hot summer day to make us forget for a little while.

Lita fell asleep. My voice droned on for a while, then

I closed the book and the bedroom door.

Finally to bed. The sinister creaking through the house quieted. The breeze through the high window cooled my head. Fatigue fastened on me, as well as Lita's arms. She held me as though she knew I wanted to get away.

I had to wait. My eyes kept closing. I would jerk myself wide awake and Lita's arms would wind tighter. "Paul, are you asleep?"

"Yes, honey. Are you?"

There was laughter in her whisper. Some of the cold fear around my heart loosened. "I had to have you with me tonight. Am I a pig?"

I kissed the tip of her nose, "You're a sweet, selfish little pig." Then I remembered my plan. "Go to sleep, baby."

She sighed—like sound tumbling downstairs. Again— lower. I lay perfectly still, waiting for her arms to drop away from me. Sounds in the hall. Who the devil was prowling around? I would have to wait for them too. Beauty snarled—just once. His evil temper was like the menace hanging over us, always there, ready to break out into vicious action.

It might have been an hour and it might have been only five minutes. I tried to slip out of Lita's embrace. She stirred and renewed her grip on me.

It would be morning and light before I knew it. I made another effort. There was no use. Finally I whispered something in her ear. She murmured sleepily, "All right," and let her arms fall loose.

I felt for my slippers while I tied my robe on. Then I opened the door into the living-room. I was relieved to hear the sound of rhythmic breathing. My hand went to my robe pocket where I had placed the ivory handle and the earring. I moved stealthily to the door and out into the hall. Beauty lurked, a foreboding ball of evil, in the far end of the hall. I waited to hear him howl a protest. He had become a person to me—an evil, unwholesome person. Only his eyes, twin points of hate, showed in the gloom, but I could picture the angry puff of him.

He made no sound. Neither did I as I dropped on down the back stairs. Then I waited. Nothing was alive down there. I slipped the bolt and closed the door carefully behind me.

There was no moon, but the stars twinkled. Shrubs made ghostly patterns, like shrouded ladies, across the lawn. My hand touched the trowel under the step. Then it was easy to find the spot I had thought of—close to the house, almost under one of our windows—a spirea bush that was lacy with bloom.

I dug to the length of the trowel. Dropped in the earring and then the carved piece of ivory. Then I smoothed over the top of the surrounding ground. If anybody thought of searching there— The trowel flipped over something white . . . the relief at dropping the evidence was replaced by fear. A pair of white gloves!

Lita had said, "My white gloves are gone." Before that

she had said, "The ivory back scratcher is gone."

I made no attempt to sort out my thoughts. In a panic I choked them down. Crushing the gloves in my pocket, I hurried around to the back door. Forgetting the need for silence, I threw in the trowel and stepped up on the porch.

Two steps and I stood paralyzed. A glinting revolver was poked almost in my face.

CHAPTER ELEVEN

THE REVOLVER WAS steady—steadier than I was—and even my heart had stopped. I had never faced a revolver before. Looking back, my life had been calm and sweet. The taste of it was in my mouth, the scent of it in my nostrils. Any minute, a slug would hurl itself through my brain. I would be like a clock from which the works have burst.

Lita! There would be nobody to help her. The police would come. I tried to get my tongue down from the roof of my mouth. It was stuck with cement—the cement of fear.

This was the murderer standing within the door, his body not visible to me. It must be Phillips. I couldn't imagine Oglesbie holding a revolver that steady, or even holding a revolver at all. It couldn't be George. He was no killer.

142

My nerves were screaming for action—anybody's action! I wanted to shout to him to shoot and get it over with.

I must have made some movement; maybe the breeze stirred me. A gruff voice said, "Make one move and you're dead!"

That voice—I had heard it—but I couldn't be sure. It came again, angry, "Who are you?"

If I hadn't been paralyzed by fear I would have shouted. I tried to say something. It wasn't a shout when it came out—it was wheezy like the speech of an old man. "It's me, Clancy. Redfern."

I had never met the wrath of Clancy before. "You damn fool! What the devil do you mean . . . ?" His voice shook. "I was just about to pull the trigger. Bouncing up on the stoop that way! Get in here before I change my mind! Scaring the life out of an old man that way . . ." His anger spent itself. He pulled out a blue bandanna and blew his nose vigorously.

I managed a squeaky, "Aren't you mixed up? I was the scared one. I still am."

He motioned me ahead of him into the dining-room. I fell into a chair and Clancy did likewise. He mopped his brow with the handkerchief. Then he grinned. "I was that scared—if the Chief had so much as an inkling, I'd have my nights for sleep and my days for puttering in the garden."

I handed him a cigarette. He inhaled the smoke, "I don't often indulge . . . but if there was so much as a drop of whiskey about?"

"I know the very place, Clancy." I walked boldly into the kitchen and lifted the bottle from behind the rolled oats. If he'd sent me for the oats, I'd never have found them. I took a couple of glasses and went back to the dining-room. "This is on Mrs. Selton. You don't mind, do you?"

He didn't hesitate. "She was a good woman. She wouldn't mind." He downed his drink and refused any more. "We don't want to be drinking it up from her. A sociable drink is in order, though, and we've had it. She won't mind that."

"After all, Clancy, some snooping dick will probably lift it. She won't need it any more."

"I'm not so sure. She may not be wanting anything to eat. But if I had her work to do I'd be wanting a nip of something. It's hot work racing through the house with me at her heels."

I took another drink under Clancy's noncommittal gaze. I had to walk up the stairs. "What are you talking about, Clancy?"

He leaned over, his hearty face close to mine. "She's haunting the place!"

"Come now, Clancy. Surely you don't believe that?"

He didn't waver. "I do. You may know a lot of things in that laboratory, but if you tried to explain them to me, they would sound like witchcraft. You believe them because somebody wrote a book on them and put names to them. Well, I've seen some funny things in my day too. But I've never been as close to the dead as I was tonight.

"Poor soul, she was floating up the stairs. I seen her when I opened my eyes. And not knowing, with the sleep still in me, I shouted and went after her. Then I seen the floating stuff she wore at her neck. It stopped me cold.

"I made the Sign of the Cross, hoping she would go back. But she didn't. She went on up. And just at the head, she turned once to look at me." Clancy reverently made the Sign of the Cross. "If I ever saw a tortured look on a soul's face before! It stilled the heart in me . . . I wanted to beg her pardon, to tell her that I wouldn't be bothering her, but my tongue was that thick!"

I didn't know what to say. I poured him a drink. He drank it unprotestingly. "Could it have been somebody else, Clancy—masquerading?"

"It was herself. I'd swear it on a stack of Bibles. And she won't rest till this thing is solved." He spoke uneasily. "That black cat came down before I could move from the foot of the stairs. He came down like a streak—that ruff around his neck standing on end and his tail twice its usual size. I knew he'd seen her too, and she wasn't real and that's what scared him."

Beauty howled as though in confirmation. Clancy saw my look toward the closed bedroom. "I let him in there."

He howled like a wild creature on a lonely moor. Clancy and I looked solemnly at each other. Sitting there, I could believe Clancy's story. Anything could happen in that house and at night. I stood up. "Hate to leave you, Clancy, but I better go up. If Lita wakes up . . ."

"Sure. Don't worry her." I hated to leave him. It was a lonely business sitting through the night in a haunted house of murder. Now Clancy would be afraid to doze off. He made his voice sound hearty. "Put the bottle where you found it. I wouldn't be offending anybody."

When I got back from the kitchen Clancy was bending his head over the sports page in the *Daily Record*. He raised his head. "You didn't say what you were doing outside tonight."

"I know, Clancy." I stuffed my hand in my pocket where there wasn't much room. The white gloves, dirt clinging to them. For almost a half hour I had been able to forget. My head ached with the return of memory. He must have known I was lying. "I went out for a breath of air."

"And I never seen you."

"Thank you, Clancy."

Going up the front stairs, where the ghost of Mrs. Selton had disappeared, I kept thinking of Clancy, as fine a cop as ever lived—more than that, as fine a man. It wasn't easy for him to break any of the regulations. But he was willing to give us a break—Lita and me—because he believed in our innocence. The ache in my head increased.

When I opened the door, both girls were staring round-eyed at me. They were standing apart but evidently they had got some comfort from being together. "Paul!" Lita said accusingly. "Where on earth?"

"Take it easy, honey. I was just down talking to Clancy."

"But why?"

My eyes shifted away from her. "I was restless. I couldn't sleep, that's all."

"Paul, your hands are dirty. You've been . . ."

"For God's sake, Lita! What if they are? It's past midnight . . . let's get to bed."

Carol's face was white with fear. "I heard a noise and got up. I didn't want to waken you." Contempt struggled with her fear. "I went over to the window and looked out. I saw somebody sneaking through the shrubbery. I was so frightened I went to your door and called." She was getting to be a nuisance. "Was it you, Paul?"

They were both staring at my hands, the nails of the left one clogged with black dirt. I couldn't make out what was in Lita's face. She was breathing raggedly, a succession of emotions flooding her lovely features. I knew that she must feel terrible.

I went over and took her in my arms. "You shouldn't be up, honey. Get back to bed." She was shivering under my touch.

Carol was getting out of hand again. "I can't stay here! I felt it! I knew I shouldn't! George made me! I can see it now . . . you both hated my grandmother! You're doing things now to cover up. I won't stay here!"

I got to the door before she did. I took her shoulders firmly in my hands. If she didn't quit screaming she would have the whole house up. My voice was bitter enough to frighten her. "I'll slap you down if you don't quit that shouting! Whatever I've done is none of your damn business, and you can make the most of it if you like! We've tried to be kind to you, but any time you want to leave, go ahead." I stood away from the door, adding, "Clancy saw your grandmother floating up the stairs. She's probably out there now, waiting to talk to you."

She backed away from the door, holding Lita's robe tight about her slim body. "I don't want to go, Paul." Her submission should have touched my heart, but it didn't. She was too willing to turn on us at the slightest chance. I complied with her, "Lock the door, will you, Paul?"

She was trying to make amends through her tears. "I didn't mean it, Paul. I'm so frightened I go all to pieces." She went closer to Lita. "You know I don't mean it, don't you, Lita?"

Lita is instinctively kinder than I. "I know it, Carol. Get in bed, dear. We all have to watch our tempers now." She smiled at me. "Coming, Paul?"

"Soon as I wash my hands." I watched the two girls slip into their beds before I turned to the bathroom. You get that way when you turn to deviousness. The door locked, back of the tub was a loose board where a plumber sometimes tinkered with the pipes. They had always been too stubborn to be affected by his indifferent wrenchings—now they could hold the gloves that might be Lita's. I washed my hands and went to bed.

Lita didn't say anything—she just twined her arms around me. I kissed her soft lips and held her close.

I don't know when she went to sleep. I was asleep as soon as I closed my eyes. Even the dreams that soon claimed me were better than reality.

Morning and a New England freshness. Sharp and clean, like a Puritan conscience that would later be heavy with heat and dismay.

We didn't have long to wait. We had had oranges and I had made coffee and toast, teasing Lita about the darkening bruise on her cheek. We both insisted on the light mood, our love for each other naked in our eyes.

The officer of the day before pounded on the door and advised us to be at Watson's Funeral Home, 11 Magazine Street. "How about my wife? She isn't supposed to come, is she?"

He grinned at me. "So his nibs says. Bring her in a cab."

Anger rose in me like hot phlegm. "But he said yesterday that she should stay in bed!"

His grin widened. "That's a record for him. He can go faster than that. We call him Jesus Christ on a roller coaster. You better have her there, and pronto." The grin was gone.

He was still there when I closed the door.

"We have to go to the morgue. Think you can make it?"

She stared unbelieving back at me. Then she moved

her feet to the floor. Her body trembled as she stood up. I was cursing the Inspector viciously to myself. Lita looked over at me. "Better hurry, Paul. Do you mind running my tub?"

"I won't do it! I'll call up the doctor. That devil can't . . ."

Her face was drained of color as she held onto the headboard. "Please, Paul." She gave me a direct look. "It will look strange if I don't go."

My eyes pulled away from her. I walked in to fill the tub.

It wasn't charming at the morgue. There were no flowers, no sanctified atmosphere to make us feel that God's will had been done. I made Lita sit down. We were all there—all of us hating it and each other. Carol, who had evidently slipped out of our rooms as soon as it was light enough to down her fear of night prowlers, kept her chin high. George was boarded up securely. Oglesbie was nervous. Brundage and Lovelace were furious at this new indignity. Phillips must have been interrupted on his way to the d.t.'s.

Lita was called in first. I grabbed her arm but she put my hand off and tried to smile. Brundage whispered something to Miss Lovelace. The others stared fixedly at Lita as she walked gracefully to the door that was waiting. Not if she died for it would she let them see the agony she suffered.

It seemed so long before she came out. I couldn't sit still

with all those hateful faces watching me. Poor Lita. What
was that demon doing to her? I tried to forget everybody
in the room as I walked the few feet back and forth.

I hurried toward her when the door opened. The Inspector stood there too. He should have died from the look
I gave him. Because Lita was on the verge of collapse. I
wasn't misled by the ghost of a smile she gave me. Underneath the bright paste, her lips were blue.

Before I could castigate him, Phillips had been beckoned
in and the door closed. He didn't even have the decency to
let me go in next, so that I could take Lita home.

A horrible thought took hold of me. Perhaps he wouldn't
let her go home. I looked around the hateful walls of the
morgue. A cell would be stronger and even more bleak.
Then I looked at Lita and hurried for a glass of water.
She drank it gratefully. I handed her a cigarette. She
reached for it and then shook her head. I knew it was
because her hands were so shaky. She wasn't going to let
them see.

The Inspector called me then. I strode toward him, murder in my eye. He was bland as usual. "We won't keep
you long, Redfern."

I was in front of the body—one of the bodies. Every
nerve in my body jumped as the sheet was whisked off.
Had it been a normal death, or even a suicide, all traces
of her last gasping moments would have been removed.
Here, they were intensified. It was just that nothing had
been done. The blood had been left in to choke the

stiffening veins. The protruding tongue was black with
it. The brown eyes protruded in a thick glaze. Had I
been the murderer I know I would have been a jibbering
maniac in two seconds. As it was, I felt my legs trembling
like pipe stems and my stomach rose up into my mouth.

The air was too close, the stench of death filled my
nostrils. My hand went to my collar, loosened the button
before I choked. I shifted my tie nervously over the space.

"Interesting, isn't it?" His eyes were amused when I was
able to lift my gaze to his.

"What do you want of me?"

"Nothing much. This is our usual procedure. It would
expedite the investigation—as well as your own discomfort
—if you would jog your memory for any bits of information that you may have forgotten before—some scraps that
may seem unimportant, even personal."

My eyes went back to the horrible corpse—I had to put
them some place. "Even personal"? What was he getting
at?

I couldn't look at the corpse any longer. I looked boldly
into his ferret eyes. "I don't know anything more!"

"Very well. You may go."

"You mean I can leave now, and take my wife?"

"Why not?" He would have laughed in my face if his
laugh muscles hadn't been atrophied. I walked out like a
robot, expecting every minute to be yanked back and
tossed onto a slab.

I took Lita's hand and we walked out into the sunlight.

It was a lovely day. There had never been a lovelier. I wanted a swim in ice cold water to cleanse myself and prove that I was alive. Instead I hailed a cab and we got out at the house and walked up that brick path.

Beauty was there. His baleful eyes watched us enter. When he was sure it was only us, his tail switched menacingly and he started that interminable howling. Lita shivered. "I don't know how much longer we can stand that, Paul."

Her nerves were stretched to the breaking point. Phillips eyed us from his door. "Come in and have a drink?"

"Thanks, Phillips. My wife isn't feeling well."

He chuckled. A whiskey chuckle. "A shot of this will make her forget. Maybe the lady ain't ever seen a corpse before. It didn't faze me. I cut a woman down once who'd been dead for three weeks. If you think this old dame smelt . . ."

Lita slumped against our door. I yelled at Phillips, "Shut up, you fool!" unlocked the door and carried her in.

"I'm so sorry, Lita."

"It's all right."

She was game as I got her clothes off and got her into bed. My own internal organism was heaving like a rough sea—I could imagine how she felt. She closed her eyes and sank down on the pillow. "I'll make some strong tea."

She nodded, her lips smiling.

The tea helped. Lita sat up to drink hers. Soon she felt like talking, nervous, disjointed talk. But I didn't try to stop her. "I never thought I could feel so weak. Maybe tomorrow I can sit down in the yard in the sun. Don't ever mention Phillips to me again, Paul. Wasn't the Inspector queer?"

"No queerer than usual. I'd hate to have to choose between him and Phillips."

"At least the Inspector wouldn't murder any one."

"He does a pretty good job of squeezing the life out of them. What do you suppose he's angling for now but somebody's life?" I wished I hadn't said it.

"But that's different. That's his job."

I changed the subject. "I'll work in the garden tomorrow while you sun yourself."

"Dig around the shrubs?"

"Of course not." Why had she said that? "The tomatoes need a lot of work on them."

She wasn't listening to me. "Paul, the Inspector asked me if I was wearing earrings the night that Mrs. Selton was murdered."

I hadn't been aware that I was gaping at her. "Close your mouth, Paul. It makes you look stupid."

I managed to say, "What did you tell him?"

"No, of course."

I must have still been looking stupid. "Paul! What is the matter with you?"

"Nothing, I guess."

"Do you suppose that he thinks only a woman wearing earrings could have committed the murder?"

"I don't know what he thinks."

I sat on the edge of the bed, dazed, afraid to move for fear I would start thinking. I heard the others coming in downstairs. I raised my eyes to Lita.

She was asleep.

CHAPTER TWELVE

I EASED MYSELF up from the bed. My heart swelled as I looked down on Lita. There was a faint flush on her bruised cheek. She looked poignant, like a little girl lost some place. I wanted to lean over and kiss away the strained look that tightened her flawless skin, flawless even with the black and blue stain.

It was better to go out and close the door. She needed rest. Walking swiftly about the living room that held Lita in every piece of stiff furniture, I crushed down the thoughts that bulged in my brain. Had the Inspector known that I had picked up the earring? He couldn't know that I had buried it. Unless Carol had told him that I had been out in the shrubbery after dark and that my hands were stained with dirt.

The earring couldn't have been significant to him—with

the other odds and ends in my pocket. He was like a ferret
—his nose could smell blood—flesh. And his brain was
sharp enough to add. If Carol told and Clancy denied seeing me—what would that do to Clancy? The Inspector
had seen Clancy rush to our defense. Would his integrity
be questioned? His income shut off? Clancy had a son
overseas. The wife and children lived with them. Two
other sons were in the Service.

I bumped into a claw-foot table, almost upsetting the
lamp. I was feeling more like a heel every minute. But
there was Lita. If I made a clean breast to the Inspector
he would drag her to a cell.

Lita had disappeared that first night! All of us were
frightened to death but she had gone downstairs. Thinking it over—her excuse was slim—to see about Beauty.
She'd had time to toss the gloves under the bush. There
wasn't a chance that anybody would ever look under the
shrubs. My head was aching but logic insisted—pushed up
sharply. When she came back she had announced that her
gloves were gone!

My head was throbbing at the effort to suppress these
alien thoughts. When somebody knocked I went gladly
to the door. Phillips stood there, a simpleton grin on his
face. "How about it now, Mac? I says to myself, 'There's
a boy who needs a drink.' And I'm the buddy who can
give it to you."

I went to his room with him. Why not? Nobody had
bothered to do anything for him. The room was a shambles

of twisted linen and tossed bottles. He poured a stiff drink into a dirty glass and handed it to me. He was loquacious even before he downed his. "Boston always has it, war or no war. You can always get a flop in Boston and a drink. That's the only thing brings me back.

"You look green around the gills, Mac. You think too much. One of them bookish fellows— You ought to get out to sea—have a tin fish spill you cursing into the ice. Or have a shark snap off your buddy's leg before you can pull him on the raft. Then you hear him scream nights, worse than that devil of a black cat. You're glad when he turns green and bloated so you can slide him back to the sharks. It's the noise." It was hard to tell whether he meant the bitter yowls Beauty was delivering or the screams of his dying buddy.

He half filled my glass. "Drink it down. And quit thinking. I killed a man once. I wouldn't think about it afterwards and they never thought of me. The dirty bastard needed killing."

"Did you ever kill a woman?"

He wasn't as drunk as I thought he was. He lunged at me. "Damn you! Don't you ever say that! I killed a man, not a woman."

I thought then that he must have killed a woman. Maybe I wanted to think that, so that it would be easy to imagine his killing . . . He was explaining, "He was riding me all the time. It was a schooner, out for fish. A big blow." His crafty eyes looked triumphant. "I picked him up by his bandy legs and cracked his skull on the taffrail before tossing him overboard. I went below and got a good shot of rum and wiped it clean out of my mind. They thought he had been hit by the boom and tossed silly."

I felt sick to my stomach. I set the glass down and got up. "You're a good guy, Mac. That's why I'm telling you this. If your skirt done in the old lady, lay low and keep mum."

My mind cleared. "My wife had nothing to do with the murder of Mrs. Selton."

"I know. I know. That's the way to talk. You got something on me, now. Don't think I'll spill the beans."

"Listen, Phillips, I'll smash you in the face if you don't shut your trap."

He still could have made mincemeat of me but he didn't move. He wiped the grin off his mouth with the back of his dirty hand. My mind was still clear as I watched him. As clean as the streets when an icy wind lashes the curb. "Why did you leave your woman hanging three weeks before you cut her down?"

He was on his feet, his tough face snarling. "Who told you? How did you know?"

"You told me."

He sat down, the wind suddenly out of him. "I did?" His eyes were unbelieving. "I never told nobody before. She made me do it. She betrayed me." I poured him a drink from his bottle. He drank it down.

I said, "Why didn't you cut her down before?"

"How the devil could I? I was out to sea. She did it twice before and I got there in time. We had a storm. I was three weeks overdue. She thought they'd fasten it on me but she stunk to high heaven. I had my papers to show."

I felt as ruthless as the Inspector—but I felt dirty too. Why should I stir up the cesspool that was this man's record? He could have killed Mrs. Selton. I knew that already. But why would he want to kill her? Even he had to have a motive. "You passed Mrs. Selton's door your first day ashore?"

"So what? The cat can look at the queen—a sailor can go past the house of a rich bitch. Get out! You don't know how to get drunk."

I went out and closed the door. He was right. What business did I have interrogating him? Even the stale air in the hall was pure compared to his air. I crossed over and opened our door. Poor Lita. Leaving her alone.

She was awake when I opened the bedroom door. She smiled at me—the sort of smile that's more sad than anything. "You're back, Paul. I couldn't imagine where you were."

"Chewing the fat with Phillips. He asked me in for a drink."

"You came in once and went out again, didn't you?"

"No, Lita. I've been in with him all the time. Why, did somebody come in?"

"Yes. I called, thinking it was you. When you didn't answer, I dozed off again." Her voice quavered. "I was so tired."

"Lita! I'm going down and buy a bolt for the door."

She sat up straight. "But why, Paul? What would anybody want in here? Who do you think it was?"

"I don't know." Of course, it might have been one of the Inspector's men snooping around. It couldn't have been Phillips. It might have been the doctor. "Perhaps it was Carol. She probably didn't want to talk. But I think we ought to keep our door bolted at night and when you're alone.

"Think you can stand it without me for a few more minutes? I won't be long."

I locked the door after me and put the key in my pocket. Then I knocked on Oglesbie's door. He finally came to the door, closed it and questioned me with his glance. Strange duck. But there was no reason why he should ask me in—I had never shown any fondness for his company. "Were you looking for me, Oglesbie?"

"No. Is there any reason I should?"

"I wondered. Somebody came in while I was out. My wife called from the bedroom but they didn't answer."

"That hardly seems characteristic of me, does it, Redfern?"

"As a matter of fact, it doesn't." The dirty little swine—thinking he had a reputation as a lady-killer. "That's all, Oglesbie, thank you. Sorry I took you away from your magnum opus."

"I have an orderly mind. I can pick up the thread immediately." He glanced back at our closed door. "You're sure your wife won't be lonesome?"

My hand was on the stair rail. "I'm not at all sure. But she is extremely discriminating."

His amused chuckle followed me down and out of that hated house. The heat of the street was a hot slap in the face. The hottest June Boston had experienced in forty years. What difference did it make? I was too numb to care whether it was hot or cold. I went hell-bent down the street. Getting a bolt to shut some of the house out was a fine errand. We could sit behind it and listen to the creakings and croakings of the old house and its inmates.

Poor Lita. I promised to take her down in the garden. It wouldn't be cooler but it would be a change of scene. All day looking at that tortured mahogany. We would have some supper; then I could put cushions in the lawn chair . . .

Bolts were hard to get. I finally found a sturdy one in a second-hand store. Scrambling through a barrel of odds and ends for the screws. Then back up Brattle.

Lita was still sitting in the same spot. "Rather interesting being locked in, Paul. There have been knocks and rattles on the door knob."

"That swine Oglesbie. He thinks he's Casanova. I'll break his head for him some day."

"Let's be genteel tonight, Paul. I feel like a convalescent.

You must amuse me. You haven't kissed me for the longest time."

"I felt too foul after I'd been in with Phillips—whiskey and rot-gut talk. Promise not to swoon, and I'll kiss you now."

"You *have* a breath, haven't you?"

"Yes. If you don't mind I'll take a cold shower as soon as I get this bolt on." I turned the screws with the can opener. Nobody came. Nobody bothered. They only seemed to come when I was out. Beauty was in the hall, carrying on, more desperate this time than any time I had heard him.

"Let him in, Paul."

"But why? He won't be any happier in here."

"I want him. I'm bored. Put him on the bed while you take your shower."

I opened the door and grabbed him before he had time to bite me. I set him down on the bed. To my surprise he didn't move, not even when Lita reached over to pet him.

"I'll be damned! There's no understanding women or cats." I heard Lita's laughter as I closed the bathroom door. I was glad she had something to laugh about.

The tingling water gave me back my youth. I stayed under a long time, thinking of what we would have for supper. Sketchy meals under my management. Salami sandwiches, dill pickles and cold beer.

When I came out Lita was petting Beauty. She had managed to tie her red ribbon, that had been holding the blonde locks out of her eyes, around Beauty's neck. He stood the indignity with great calm. "Well, you ought to be with Beatty—you're a lion tamer. "

"I feel too frustrated to be a lion tamer. Carol was here. She wanted those letters."

"Well, did she get them?"

"No. They weren't here."

"She's crazy! They're right in that drawer." I crossed over and opened the highboy. They weren't on top where they had been. I went all through the junk. "That's funny. They were right there."

"She accused me of hiding them."

I looked at Lita. She was more amused than angry, stroking Beauty with long even strokes of her shapely hands. I was still dumb over his docility. She said, "I never saw anybody change like Carol. She was so sweet when she came."

"Things haven't been too slick for her. I suppose it's natural that she should think we're all against her. But I'm surprised that she should think you want the letters.

"Well, I'm going to lock you in again and go to the store."

"I'm beginning to feel like a beauty in a locked castle."

Somebody had taken the letters. Was it Oglesbie? Who would want them besides Carol? That bolt was a good idea. At least no one could prowl around our rooms at night. The ghost get-up was a good murder masquerade. Keep Clancy rooted to the spot. If you saw the ghost of Mrs. Selton in your rooms at night, you wouldn't be apt to investigate. A man or a woman could wear the disguise.

We had our supper. Even Lita didn't want to go down to the garden and run the gauntlet of Carol's animosity. It was pleasant being alone. Even Beauty was attractive in his new attitude. I fed him milk and some liver I got for him. He was ravenous. "Don't you think that ribbon bothers him?"

"He didn't like it at first, but that's what seems to have tamed him."

As Phillips said, when I didn't think, I was all right. Lita bathed and I washed the dishes. Then we played pinochle with a dummy hand and listened to the radio. We didn't talk of anything important.

We were both ready for bed by ten o'clock. Beauty was already comfortable on the foot. Lita remembered, "I wonder if Carol is coming up."

"Let her stay down there." I tucked Lita in. When I stooped over to kiss her, her eyes dilated. She screamed.

I turned quickly. Lovelace, like a black wraith, was standing almost at the foot of the bed. Beauty gave a snarl and jumped off the bed and out the door like a streak.

I was sore. Didn't any of these people have the decency to knock? It's true I hadn't locked up yet, but the door was closed. "We didn't hear you knock, Miss Lovelace."

She looked as woeful as a lost sheep. "Amy is right. I am getting absent-minded. I do apologize."

"That's all right." I was instantly contrite. The poor old thing was half batty with all the excitement. She took the chair I shoved forward. "I was here twice before and nobody answered."

So that was who it was. "I thought you would be in bed by this time. It hasn't been a pleasant day except for the weather."

She sighed deeply. "Amy is in bed. But I could not sleep if I did retire. I have had a great many things to think about." This hardly seemed the time for her to make small talk but we put up with it. She was so white that I was sure she must be ill. She usually had rosy cheeks and a serene look in her eyes. The old coquette must have used make-up.

Her tone became sepulchral. "I came to extend an invitation."

Lita hadn't spoken. She did now, her face lighted up. "That's lovely of you, Miss Lovelace. I've had to stay in bed and I've been bored to tears. Out West, I always rode horseback and swam and hiked besides my dancing, but since we've been here, Paul has been so busy. I've never had to stay in bed before—not that I remember . . ."

Lovelace was watching her. There was a sort of bitterness on her face that I had never seen before. Did she think that Lita had something to do with Mrs. Selton's cruel death? I shook myself free from my thoughts. I mustn't watch everybody with an eye to their suspicions of Lita. Lita didn't deserve that.

"I am sure you have led a very active life, out West. It would be distressing if you were ever confined."

"What do you mean—have a baby?"

Miss Lovelace stood up, everything on her quivering with indignation. "I'm not interested in your possibilities as a breeder. I said I came to extend to you and your husband an invitation."

"Yes, I know." Lita's voice was contrite.

"It is an invitation to attend the funeral services for my late friend, Mrs. Selton."

We were both silent, for a long while. Then I found myself gibbering like a perturbed monkey. "I didn't know they would—they would permit a service until—"

Her face, prim now in its austerity, overpowered me. "Until the murderer is found?"

I nodded my head.

"I think they have found the murderer."

We didn't move or speak while she swished sedately to the door and disappeared. Then I ran over and locked and bolted it.

CHAPTER THIRTEEN

Sleep took over. And nightmares. I was running to an open grave with the black cat. He was snarling—trying to get there first. He was a bloated evil wild thing that I couldn't outrun. My legs ached with the effort. They were heavy with weakness, spindly—while the black cat became monstrous in size. In the grave was Lita. She was dead.

I bolted out of bed, my hair almost on end with fright. Lita clutched at the sheet I'd twisted from her. She started to exclaim, "Pa—" I sounded a warning to silence her. Because the knob of our door was turning. I could hear the creaking. The door was bolted but right then the bolt gave me no sense of security.

I moved my legs, made them go toward the door in the darkness. Picking up the brass candletick, I turned the key, shoved the bolt back and opened the door. The hall was dark—there wasn't even the blue dimness. Something bulky stood there. I raised the candlestick . . .

"Not so fast, boy."

My arm fell limp, the candlestick fell to the carpet. It was Clancy, his voice serious. "Come in, Clancy. I wouldn't want to dent your head. I don't know who I thought it was."

"No, I'll not be coming in. I knocked—but I didn't want to wake the others. There's been another murder."

I tried to stare into his face—all I could see was a blur of whiteness. I stood there not able to believe it. Which one was it? Another murder?

"Will you be coming down with me?"

"Yes, Clancy." My feet were bare. I had only my pajamas. But I followed Clancy down the hall to the front stairs. He wasn't asking me—he was telling me to follow him. The shock had been sufficient to strain the kindness from Clancy's voice.

It was almost like my nightmare following him down the stairs, his feet heavy. He stopped halfway down. My body bumped against him. In the blue light of the lower hall, his face was stony.

"Is it down there, Clancy? Who . . ."

"Lean over."

I wondered if Clancy was being affected by the house of death—alone through the night—people falling down stairs, ghosts prowling about and Beauty raising holy hell. Because I leaned over the rail and the hall was empty.

"Look again," Clancy said. He pointed as though it were under the stairs. I leaned over. My eyes grown used to the darkness now, I saw it.

My hands clutched the balustrade, unbelieving.

There, hanging by a red silk ribbon, swung the inert body of Beauty. I felt my stomach heave as I looked down into the bared teeth, the helpless claws. He wouldn't howl through the halls, the rooms, any more—the smoky Persian had been murdered. I agreed with Clancy—this was murder.

Clancy stood there, not looking down, his wrath formidable. I said, "Lita wanted to bring him into our rooms tonight. If I had let her—this wouldn't have happened. It was strange that he let her pet him. I never thought he would. She detested him once, but after Mrs. Selton's death she felt sorry for the poor beast."

In the face of Clancy's silence I felt obliged to run on with words. Behind the jumbled facade of words, I was ticking off the people in the house. None of us, except Lita who was moved by pity, liked him. Carol seemed to at times, but he wouldn't let her touch him. Lovelace had tried to be nice. Phillips had killed a man. What would a cat—especially a cat that howled at night—be to him? Just something to get rid of. The ribbon had been around his neck where Lita had put it. It was there for anybody who wanted to stretch it tight. Beauty would snarl, but what chance would his viciousness have against a man sixteen times his size?

A coat or cloth twisted around the black cat's body and he would be helpless!

I was putting my conviction into words, almost as angry now as Clancy. "Whoever murdered that cat—murdered Mrs. Selton!"

"That is what I'm thinking."

I was thinking of Phillips. He wouldn't wear gloves. He would do the job quickly and forget it. "This may help solve Mrs. Selton's murder. There may be fingerprints . . ." Then I thought of Lita. Her fingerprints would be on the ribbon—that red stretch of silk so like the flaming scarf that choked the breath of Mrs. Selton.

"Yes. I better call the Inspector."

He moved down—a step or two closer to the stiffening black body. I couldn't move. We would be in for it. The Inspector would come. He would question Lita. It seemed that every act we did, every innocent move sunk us deeper into the mire of our landlady's murder.

Clancy was looking at me, his face a blur before my eyes. "I won't be saying anything about Mrs. Redfern being on the stairs."

His voice was low. It was kind. But I couldn't make sense to the words. He went on, "The one who murdered the cat is a killer. He may be insane but I don't think so. He is just a killer. I've seen it, over and over. When a grown person can kill an animal in cold blood for no reason at all, he will kill anything."

"What did you say, Clancy, about Lita on the stairs?"

"It was only that she came a few feet down. It must have been a couple of hours ago. She wanted to know if I'd seen Beauty. And I told her I hadn't seen hide or hair of him all night. That the devil must have got him. I wouldn't have said that if I'd known.

"It will be after upsetting the Inspector if I tell him that, and it has no bearing on the case."

"Clancy! Tell the Inspector! I appreciate everything. But we can't hide behind your back. You have your job and your family to consider."

He gave a quick glance at the hanging cat and turned his back on the brutal fact of it to pick up the phone. Before he dialed he said without emotion, "You might tell her what I said. The Inspector is a fine man but he's like a rat terrier I once had—he'd go for kittens as well as rats and when he quit shaking them they were like the chaff when the wheat is threshed."

His heavy fingers found the dial. There were things I wanted to say to him. Again he was covering up for us. I looked from his unhappy face to the dead cat hideously swaying in the air—swing right, swing left. My feet were leaden as I went up to Lita.

Down the upper hall, calm as death itself . . . someone behind a door, hands relaxed, hate assuaged for a few hours, until the impulse to strangle again . . .

Lita was standing in the living room. She looked like someone awaiting a death sentence. One cheek still held a high yellow cast. Otherwise she was very pale. "What is it, Paul? What happened?"

I pulled the words up, laid them flat between us. "Beauty has been strangled."

Her hands fluttered, went out to hold the back of the sofa. She wasn't pale now—she was chalk white. Pity for her welled up in me. I should have been kinder. That would have to come later. "Clancy says he won't tell the Inspector that you were on the stairs tonight. He doesn't want it to be any harder for you."

"Harder for me?" She hadn't yet got it.

"He'll be here soon. Clancy called him. He seems to think that both jobs were done by the same person . . . Whoever wanted Mrs. Selton out of the way had no love for Beauty."

"Does Clancy think . . ."

I went over to her. "Of course not, darling. Would he make it easier for you if he did? You're cold as ice. Come on, get in bed." I covered her up. She was shivering. "Paul, I feel as though I had stepped in soft cement . . . now it's hard.

"Last night I thought I heard Beauty cry. I went out in the hall. When he wasn't there, I asked Clancy."

"Forget that now, darling. We haven't time. Compose yourself and don't let Clancy down. He'll have a hard enough time explaining his not seeing or hearing anything."

She couldn't stop shivering. "That was horrible—to do that to Beauty. It makes me afraid. I don't see why . . .

he was getting over her. He was going to be friendly. Oh, Paul, I wish I hadn't put that silly ribbon around his neck."

We heard a scream from the lower hall. I said, "Carol must know. That means the Inspector is here."

We waited until we heard his step in the hall. Then he was at the door. I lighted a cigarette before opening it. "Come in, Inspector."

He didn't bother with me but made straight for Lita. She met his gaze. Watching her, I couldn't have told that she was as tremulous as a bowl of jelly.

When his eyes left her face, they started taking inventory, settling finally on a wad of black fur that clung to the tufted bed covering. I hadn't seen it before. It must have fallen there when he lay on the bed the day before.

Lita saw it too. The Inspector watched her eyes widen. She didn't flinch. "Beauty was on the bed yesterday. He was so lonesome that he let me pet him. I put the red ribbon around him then . . . I never thought that anybody would . . ."

He reached over, put the black wad into a small envelope and went out of the room.

CHAPTER FOURTEEN

LITA BURST into tears. Between the racking sobs, "I'm afraid, Paul. For the first time in my life, I'm afraid! That Inspector, Paul! Did you see the way he looked at me? He thinks that I . . . that I killed . . ."

I crushed her to me. "He'll never get you, Lita! Never!"

She twisted in my arms until she could look at my face. "Why, Paul, you say that as if . . ."

I hurried on, "We have a fight on our hands, Lita. The cards are stacked against us but we've got to win! We've got to! Let's not waste time thinking of anything else."

Her voice had no life in it. "But how, Paul? He . . . he's so sure of himself. He makes my flesh creep."

I lied bravely, "He makes us all feel that way. The rest of them are shivering in their boots too. Look at George—he came back for an umbrella. His timing was unfortunate. You know how he felt toward Mrs. Selton. She kept him from getting a degree and she said things to Carol that enraged him."

"But, Paul, you know as well as I that George wouldn't . . . why, he couldn't . . ."

"Listen, Lita, we have to find the murderer. And we have to use the Inspector's methods. Each one in this house is guilty—except us, of course—until we find the real one."

"Oh, Paul, it's hopeless. What can we do?"

"I have ideas." I didn't have. "I'll rake into Oglesbie's past. And into Phillips'. Even the old gals could have done it. What do you think that hate that Brundage has nursed all these years would lead to? And Carol? You know what that accusation against her name meant to her? At that moment she hated her grandmother with a consuming passion. Don't think she didn't mention it to George as they stood there on the corner of Brattle, trying to decide."

She began to laugh hysterically. "Oh, Paul, you're precious! I suppose you will do research, at Widener?"

"That's an idea. You're damn right, I will. Listen, people don't murder out of the blue." I was pacing now. That's exactly what I would do. The newspaper stacks—why not? I stopped before Lita. "Each act in each person's life adds up . . ."

"I know—it adds up to murder. Remember, Professor, that people can murder without premeditation." Her face became ironic. "The Inspector is right. Even I could have strangled Mrs. Selton had she said the provoking remark at the psychological moment."

I stared back at her. "No, Lita. You couldn't. I don't find your attitude amusing. You have always been kind . . . why, even to that vicious Beauty!'

She laughed outright. "You don't know your murder psychology, dear. Murderers are always kind to animals, until . . ."

"Lita! For God's sake! Can't you be serious? Laugh at me if you want to, but . . ."

I saw then that her irony was only a mask for her terror. "I am only laughing at myself. If I am a murderer—I'm a very clumsy one. I've left such a trail . . .'

I thought of the earring, and the gloves. If the Inspector had those? I shook myself. "Lie back and get some rest, Lita. I'll make some coffee and then I'll give the rooms a good cleaning."

"Why, Paul? Make some coffee and come back to bed. There's no object in cleaning. Let the dust gather."

But I had to do something until the library opened. It was barely daylight, with the robins twittering in the trees and the scent of the locust blossoms faint in the still air. There was no sound in the house. The rooms seemed like a vacuum that I was forced to fill with sound and fury.

The handle of the carpet-sweeper, a pre-Civil War model, came loose. The metal bracket fell down. In yanking the bracket loose, the dirt belched out into two per-

fect oblongs of refuse. I said things about the old house
and some of its decrepit gear.

I stopped, hearing voices below in the garden. Hurrying
to the window, below me in the early dawn I saw Carol
and George. In Carol's arms was a white oblong box tied
in white satin ribbon. The remains of Beauty!

They were talking in soft tones. But I could clearly
hear. My blood pressure went up when George said,
"Under that white bush!"

I must have exclaimed, because Lita stood by me in her
thin nightdress. Her fingers clutched my arm when she
saw. We watched the two of them walk over to the
spirea—George had a spade. They stood there, Carol looking down at the box. George reached under the white
sprays with his shovel. Now! Now they would turn up
the ivory handle along with the blue earring. They would
know . . .

Carol turned, her caprice for once gratifying. "No,
George! Under the weeping willow . . . we can put flowers.
I don't want him shoved in a corner . . . neither would
Grandmother."

My breath came out in a rush. "It's all right, Lita! They
won't find anything. They won't . . ."

"Paul!" Her hand had fallen from my arm; her eyes
were wide as she studied my face, then my hands. I knew
she was remembering the dirt under the nails that night.
She turned abruptly and went back to the bed. She was
filing her nails, not looking at me. She looked so helpless,

so lovely . . .

I went on with my cleaning, the solid pieces of furniture mocking me with their rigidity. From time to time I looked at Lita. I wanted to tell her that everything would be all right. We had always been able to talk over anything. But she was reading as though I weren't in the room.

I was glad when I heard loud voices downstairs. I went to the door. Brundage was shouting, "You are not going to move your grandmother's chair. It has always stood there and that's where it is going to remain!" And Carol's answer, "I'm going to change the whole room. I can't look at things the way they are—it depresses me. And, Miss Brundage, I shall have to ask you to go up to your rooms. You have had altogether too much to say in this house!"

"Oh . . . Oh!" The old gal was breathing indignation like a boiling tea kettle as she came up the stairs. Coming out of their apartment, she was reenforced by Miss Lovelace. This ought to be good, I told the silent Lita. Miss Lovelace's voice: "We will leave everything as it is. I telephoned for Annie to come for the cleaning. She doesn't know of the tragic circumstances. I couldn't help thinking that Annie must be the only person in Greater Boston who didn't know—Annie must be deaf as well as a non-reader. Lovelace explained, "I told her that her former mistress had gone to her reward."

Simple, that. But Lovelace was continuing, "Caroline, dear, I hope you have a simple black dress that covers

your knees. We will bury your grandmother tomorrow
from this parlor. All of your grandmother's as well as your
grandfather's friends will be here. Also, I sent the notices
to the papers yesterday—the neighbors and the tradespeople
will be in. You will of course take your place at my side
in my rooms."

There was no answer from Carol. I closed our door and
went over to Lita. "Have you a good black dress that
covers your knees?"

I got her attention, a noncommittal, "Why?"

"You will be expected to wear it at the invitational
funeral tomorrow. In Miss Lovelace's rooms. You will meet
the holy friends from the Hill. I hope you can bear up."

She was indignant. "I hope she doesn't expect me to
wear a large red 'M' on my good black! Why, I think
the whole thing is in the poorest taste. I won't be present!"

Nevertheless when I left, Lita was taking out the hem of
a black dress. I kissed her goodbye. "I'll try not to be
long." Her eyes smiled at me. I felt like a knight without
armor or sword going out to boo at the dragon that was
hell-bent in our direction.

I knocked at Phillips' door. The first thing that arrested
my eyes when he stood in its opening was a bloody scratch
on his right hand. He sneered, "What the hell business
is it of yours? It's like I told the Inspector, if I'd wanted
to kill the cat I'd give it a good kick to bash its brains
out. What do you want?"

I could have told him that cats howl if you kick them.

He found it expedient to add, "I got this cut over a skirt in Scollay. Don't look so goddam pious."

That was my cue. "I just came to say that I was sorry about the way your wife died. Even after five years it must still be hard to think of the way she looked . . ."

"I wish it was five. It's only been two. I've been all over the world, South America, England, Africa, Russia, all of them, but she goes right along to share every bottle with me. Sometimes I think I'll go crazy."

"I can imagine! Well, I'll see you later, Phillips. I have to go out."

"Yes, you better go while you can." He laughed coarsely and I went down the steps and out.

Looking through newspaper stacks is a tedious job. Narrowing the time to two years ago wasn't as bad as it might be. Finally I found it. A small item in the *Traveler*. It was just as he had said. He was dismissed after his papers proved that he had been at sea. Neighbors said she was a very devout woman, almost a recluse, a member of the Mystic Yearners. It wasn't possible to think of Phillips being married to a religious fanatic. That could account for his subconscious fear now. She had punished him by hanging herself after unsuccessfully trying to re-form him. Perhaps he wasn't so tough when he was younger. And perhaps he loved the woman or had loved her.

There wasn't anything more to be found on Phillips. I took up the bloodhound act on the good doctor. I came smack up against his smug face in 1935. In some insidious manner he had wormed his way to Dr. Hrdlicka at the Smithsonian in Washington. The newspapers were interested. He didn't tell them anything about Dr. Hrdlicka but considerable about Dr. Frederick Oglesbie and his forthcoming book on skeletal material which would astound the scientific world.

The old humbug! Still writing the book. Hours later I found an item on his divorce. So he had been married? She was evidently quite young, also a student of anthropology. But she objected to his habit of hypnotizing her. I almost laughed out loud in that academic stronghold.

Then I almost tumbled over backward. A hypnotist? Could Oglesbie be a hypnotist? Had she said that merely to secure a divorce? No. I was sure of it. He had influenced Mrs. Selton. Why would she care about his damn book? She wouldn't understand a scientific or literary impulse. She had brought him home after meeting him in the subway. He might have impressed her then as one who could help her. She was always seeking something. He might even have known who she was and bent a meaningful gaze for his own sinister purposes.

She kept him in the house against the bitter opposition of her friends. They certainly never liked him. I began to understand Carol's intense hatred of him. The good doctor would need some investigation. But it was time to go back to Lita.

My smile was broad as I went down the steps of the

library. The old devil! The sinister, soft-spoken, effeminate dish of mush. Waving his soft hands and intoning, "Relax . . . Relax now . . . You will do as I say . . ."

The cigarette dropped from my fingers. Good God! I stood there in the Harvard Yard, the imposing structures of brick closing me in, while my mind grappled with the slippery thought. Silence! Complete silence that night in the old house. Mrs. Selton in her chair, quiescent, relaxed. Doing what she was told. "Open your mouth." The ivory hand eased down her throat. "Now, sit still . . . don't move." The silk scarf . . . a quick twist . . . her eyes glossing over with pitiful dismay . . . her trusting obedience while the tongue shot out for breath.

That was it. My God, that was it! It was the only way it could have been done. She was a woman of spirit. She would have fought for her life. But she had given him the power of life and death over her . . . she had submitted to his hypnotic power.

Lita! Shame covered me at the thought of her. How could I ever make it up to her? My feet dragged as I walked out into the square. I got home. A cab driver cursed me for almost running me down. I walked up the steps, across the narrow porch. Voices in the kitchen—Carol and George. Then up to our rooms.

Lita was startled at my appearance. "Paul, what happened?" She had on the black dress. It made her look older and out-of-date, with the hem longer.

I had her in my arms, stroking the honey-colored hair,

kissing her eyelids, her cheek where the bruise still lingered
her lips. She smiled up at me. "Paul, you've come back.
All the terrible things that happened built a wall between
us."

"It's down now, darling. I can see into the fog. I
know something."

A look of fright came back into her eyes. "What, Paul?
Did you really uncover something in the library?"

"Yes. Oglesbie is a hypnotist. That's why we didn't
hear any sound. He must have hypnotized her."

"Paul!" There was a trace of amusement. "He isn't the
type. He's no Svengali. I can't picture it."

"Well, I'll get it out of him tonight, somehow! Then
I'll go to the Inspector."

She drew away from me. "It seems horrible—your putting the finger on him. You may send him to the electric
chair. And it may all be just circumstantial evidence."
Her face took on a drawn, old look. "When the Inspector
looks at me with that thin smile of his, I know what it
feels like to be hunted. Don't do it, Paul! Let the Inspector
find the one!" She had her eyes covered—her shoulders
were shaking. I couldn't make it out.

I said no more. We ate. Lita had put on a flowered
housecoat—the black dress hung in the wardrobe, plainly
visible behind the glass doors. The funeral tomorrow! We
would all be there—Oglesbie too. Unless I could force the
Inspector to move. Lita was probably right—I didn't have
enough to go on yet. There was the scratch on Phillips'

hand. But the one who choked the cat wasn't necessarily the one who . . .

Lita asked me to put the radio on. I did and then said I was going in to talk to the old gals. She made no comment. When I knocked at their door, Brundage drew back in affront when she saw me. She looked terrible—could it be grief? I hardly thought so. When she had disdainfully admitted me, I could understand how anybody would feel bilious in those rooms. The gay little Dresden pieces, the velvet cushions, even the cuckoo clock had been removed. Sombre black covered everything. The shades were drawn—I could barely distinguish the two black-clad women. Their white faces looked like masks carried around on poles.

Miss Lovelace made sound come out of her mask. "We are not at home this evening."

I did manage to feel abashed. "I'm sorry. There was something I wanted to ask you."

"Yes?"

"Did Mrs. Selton mention Dr. Oglesbie in her will?"

Two shocked gasps. Miss Lovelace told me through shut lips, "Your question is tactless." Then she answered it, "She did not!"

My face fell. Then he didn't have a motive. Before it all fell to pieces I decided that he could still have strangled her if she had ordered him out of the house because of his attentions to Carol. His fawning would turn to hatred in a flash.

The mask of Brundage was quivering—it came closer. "Why do you ask? Does it concern you?"

I stood up. "You're d— you're right! It does concern me. It concerns every one of us. Somebody in this house murdered Mrs. Selton. And I intend to find out who that somebody was."

And it didn't concern me that I had thrust a false note into their mourning ritual. This was murder, and not a Dionysian orgy for emotional outlet.

That night I knocked on Oglesbie's door. It was about ten but there was no answer. Then I heard his voice below —that self-conscious laugh.

The knob yielded. I opened the door. My hand found the light switch. Then I almost died. A skull, its empty eye sockets blood red, its teeth bared, jumped up and down before my eyes. Everything else in the room was black as the inside of an underground crypt. The leering thing stopped jumping. I realized then that I was the thing that shook. My stomach was still tossing about like a rotten melon on an oily slough.

When the thing blinked off, and the darkness gathered around me, I had the impulse to bolt. Then a click and a toothier, more malevolent skull, apparently dripping blood, took its place. One after another, with a click like a snapping of yellow molars, gathered and receded before my eyes. They were made more hideous by their deformities, a piece of jaw gone in one, an eye socket cracking open, a skull fracture, gaping tooth sockets. Crimson behind the openings. As though each had been the victim of murder.

The diabolical, scheming monster! He belonged in a cage in a psychopathic ward. I knew the whole thing was a trick, but my nerves jumped as I moved toward the hideous things. I pulled on the reading lamp, stealing their thunder, making them less bloody. Then I went back and switched off the light that connected them.

A book lay open on his desk. I expected a booby trap in its pages. Perhaps if I touched it there would be an explosion. Evidently he didn't want snoopers in his room. He had something to hide. What?

I turned the pages carefully. Then I glanced up at the title, "Superstitions, Past and Present." Tame reading for him. My meagre store of courage returned. I could have laughed then, but I didn't. I was in the room of a murderer—I was sure of it.

I picked the book up. Nothing happened. There was a bookmark—a nude girl. It was a snapshot—not a professional model. Too artless, too natural. Yet no trace of self-consciousness. Her eyes—yes, I noticed her eyes in spite of the curves—looked back at me without any expression.

With the bookmark in my right hand, I looked at the page it marked. "Spiders. Spider Webs." It sounded like Oglesbie but why had he recently been reading this? I was wondering who the girl could be—she seemed too sweet a type for Oglesbie—and why he was reading up on superstitions—when my eyes refused to move.

They held fast to four words, "The Stroke of Death"!

Still numb, I read, "The hand of a dead man stroking the throat of a person with goitre . . . supposed to effect a cure."

A soft chuckle broke the silence. My head turned slowly —the doctor stood there, regarding me. He closed the door softly and came toward me, his small feet making no sound on the carpet.

CHAPTER FIFTEEN

I STARED at him as though he were the devil's emissary, but he seemed determined blandly to face it out. "I see my little lighting arrangement didn't deter you. It wasn't meant to impress a fellow scientist." His eyes hardened for a minute. "I can't say that I enjoy having people visit me in my absence. But we'll let that pass, for the present. I see you also discovered the 'Stroke of Death' reference. I was just down telling Caroline and George about it."

I was meant to feel like a snake whose venom has just been withdrawn, but I refused the role. The man was as clever as sin. I looked into his small eyes behind the pale lashes. "That was smart of you, Oglesbie. I suppose you also told the Inspector?"

"No, but I will if he is interested."

I laughed, "I think he will be. But to make sure, I'll

tell him myself, tonight."

His eyes hardened but there was bewilderment in the suddenly slack mouth. "You wouldn't do that, Redfern? Why, I intended to do all I could for your wife. You won't accomplish anything by trying to put it on me. Together, you and I . . ."

"Damn you! Don't think you can bribe me." His bland impudence was like a smack in the face. "You've gone to plenty of trouble to implicate her. Planting that ivory stroker on the body! Who else would have thought of it but you who gave it to her? Then that note that you made Mrs. Selton write! 'The Stroke of Death.' You're the Stroke of Death, you clumsy sneak! I know you hypnotized Mrs. Selton!"

His face blanched but he recovered quickly. His even teeth flashed in a contemptuous laugh. "Your fear for your wife has led you far afield. I would not advise you to go further—it might prove fatal. I've done a little investigating of my own." I watched him closely. He hadn't gone to pieces at the mention of hypnotism. Was he too clever for me?

I said, "You did use hypnosis on Mrs. Selton, didn't you?"

"Yes. But only at her request—when the inner turmoil became too great. It gave her a momentary release from her worries—I never wanted to use my power!"

He looked almost capable of hypnotic power—then. Every feature of his face was hard. He tried to draw me

away from my line of questioning. "I don't advise you
to do anything about it, but I can tell you this—Phillips
being here was no accident!"

His old tactics, drawing the red herring to somebody
else's door. I pointed my right hand at him. "Shut up about
Phillips! You hypnotized Mrs. Selton and then stuck
that hand down her throat. She didn't make a sound.
That's the only explan—"

I wasn't prepared for his reaction. His lips drew back
in a snarl that matched the fang-like striving of his hands.
The dapper little doctor in a split second flew into a rage
that kept me pointing my arm . . . When he clawed at it,
I crushed the bookmark in doubling my fist. I hit him a
gentle one on the jaw. He didn't go down. Cursing with
all of the ugly malevolence of a practised curser, he went
for my throat.

It was ridiculous that one of his size could send me
into a gasping, retching agony. His fingers were as strong
as steel wires. My eyes were open but the room swam
before me in black splotches, weaving under my feet. I
was slugging—I knew that. My fist was beating against
a bag of putty.

Finally the bag sagged, the fingers loosened, he slumped
to the floor. I was gasping for breath—humiliated. His
curses stopped when my hand opened and the bookmark
fell on his face. He tried to smooth it out, but even
making allowance for my jumping arteries, I could see
that the smooth nude would never be smooth again.

He looked up at me, the fury not out of him yet. "I'm afraid I will have to kill you, Redfern."

"It won't be your first attempt."

He was crying like a forlorn boy when I stepped over him and went in to wash up. Lita was in bed. She was reading. My hair was combed and I was washed, but she looked as frightened when she looked up from her book as though she had seen me in the clutches of a murderer. "What have you been doing, Paul?" She has a melodious voice even when it is reproving.

"Gathering evidence. I'm going to take it to the Inspector now. I want you to bolt your door when I leave."

She got out of bed slowly. "If you won't listen to me, Paul . . ." She came closer—the clean fragrance of her reminding me of warm nights . . . just the two of us . . . the willows with the Columbia slup-slupping . . . "Paul! Your throat!" Her look of terror reminded me.

I took her hands. "It was nothing, Lita. Now don't imagine things. We had a tussle but I can take care of myself. And nobody in this house will shoot or stab— they like to strangle."

She drew back. "You mean . . . Dr. Oglesbie?"

I nodded, hating the reluctance with which she accepted his guilt. "All you have to do, darling, is keep your door bolted. And I promise that I won't let him get his hands on my throat again. I'm going now, Lita." I kissed her and went out.

She didn't believe that the doctor was guilty. In spite of

the marks of his fingers on my throat!

Which was probably why I couldn't impress the Inspector. There was something to be said on his side. I had forced him to get out of bed to listen to me. I began to see why he carried the thin smile about with him—without it he wouldn't get any evidence, he'd scare the suspects to death.

"Are you quite finished, Redfern?"

He was laying me away in concrete with a thick layer of solid contempt. I didn't have to answer. He liked to talk, when he felt that way. "Your work for our division is very commendable. How far have you got in your correspondence course on detecting? Probably not far enough to realize that a murderer always leaves some little token at the scene of the crime. We have a token or two and they don't spell Oglesbie. Regarding that gentleman, we would be very glad to oblige you if the case didn't have to be tried in a court of law. But the attorney for the prosecution won't be happy if we expect him to tell a fantastic tale about dead hands and mesmerism. And the jury won't believe him unless he has some evidence linking the suspect to the crime."

I didn't mind the contempt, but "some little token at the scene of the crime" banged away in my head. "The ivory hand may have belonged to my wife, but can't you believe that somebody could have taken it and put it at the scene of the crime?"

His thin smile came into play. "Don't jump to conclusions. We don't convict anyone. All that our division does is to gather the evidence, tangible as well as intangible, and place it in the hands of the judge. It is his duty . . ."

"I don't care about his duty. What do you think it would do to my wife to be the main suspect or one of the suspects to be questioned by the judge?"

"Have I mentioned your wife? What makes you think that you aren't my main suspect?"

I didn't return his smile. I got up. "Then you don't want any more information that may come our way?"

"I will be very happy to listen. In fact, it is your duty to give us anything you know. That is, if it isn't too fanciful and in the middle of the night at the same time. And if you don't expect me to make immediate arrests."

His last remark gave me some comfort as I hailed a cab. He was keeping his mind open—just a crack. And he had made some notes while we talked. I began to feel better. But I didn't mean to leave it all to him—not by a jugful! as we Westerners say. As the taxi slid through the dark streets, my mind kept turning over the loose sod. Oglesbie? Hypnosis? He could do it. But would he kill the goose who laid the golden eggs? He could have had another ten years of easy life. Old ladies never died in Greater Boston—even old ladies with swellings on their necks. But she had been in a vile humor that night—she might have said something to anger him. When he flew at my throat he had every intention of squeezing the life out of me. Had she dragged him over the coals because of his passes at Carol, and ordered him out, he would have been capable of strangling her. And she was capable of saying some pretty nasty things. She might have had one of those aging attachments for him herself, something that she didn't quite understand. Her mind showed its warped pattern when she accused Lita of having an affair with George.

And what did Oglesbie mean by his reference to Phillips? Was there a grain of truth there? It didn't seem possible that Phillips could ever have known her. Lovelace and Brundage certainly didn't. The cab stopped and so did my thoughts.

The old house was shrouded like the old gals' rooms in dull black, its bulk brooding in the still air, awaiting the return of the woman who lay in her black box in the undertaking parlor. A taste of bile slipped over my tongue at the thought of the coming ordeal—stiff flowers, music to empty the tear ducts, the creaking joints of the old people who never came to see her when she was alive, who never helped her to find her way.

I was just morbid. The old gals were sincere in their grief. So was Carol. Lita was too. And Oglesbie, if he did it and got nothing out of it. I stepped over the threshold and closed the door. The dim blue light, nothing else. It might have been a piece of shiny paper for all the light it gave.

My God! How did Clancy spend his nights alone in that pregnant atmosphere? The stiff drapery whispered

faintly as I stood, accustoming my eyes to the dim blue-
ness. Musty age filled my nostrils. "Clancy?" I said softly.
No use waking the poor fellow up, to sit through the
night in . . .

The ceiling crashed down on me . . . I could see the
stars in bursting splendor, ear-splitting as they rushed
. . . then darkness with the roaring.

Lita was moaning. I tried to get up. Water splashing on
my face. Clancy's voice, awed and respectful. "It was herself. I saw her. *They* don't like it if you spy on them, so
I took myself to the back stoop."

The pounding in my head was like a riveting machine
as the arteries sent the blood through the shocked channels.
Somebody had hit me. *Herself* indeed? My hand moved
to wipe away the water. It kept coming. I opened my eyes
—Lita's tears, as she bent over me. Her face twisted with
grief. "Paul! Oh, Paul!"

Clancy was still concerned with ghosts. "You should
never go in a room where *they* are, my boy, not after
midnight."

I raised myself, my hands holding my head together.
Lita said, "Call a doctor, Clancy."

"No!" I didn't want to sound so mean, but my head
was split in two. "I'll be all right." I stood up, brushing
them away. Lita came back. She clung to me just as I was
about to crumble. Then Clancy with a stout arm held me
up lop-sided. I was swearing. Lita was trying to reason
with me. "You have to have a doctor, Paul. Don't be

stubborn."

"I won't have a doctor. If my skull is cracked maybe I can wrestle with ghosts and not go falling on my face."

"It's a bit of respect you need and more staying in your room," said Clancy severely.

"Okay. Let's go." Then my mind began to work rationally. I made a lunge for the drapery, dragging my support with me. I looked as foolish as Don Quixote at a windmill as my face hit the wood behind. Clancy, with a strong arm, pulled the stiff tapestry aside. Nobody there.

We went upstairs, my feet dragging like a drunk's. Oglesbie's door opened a crack. He stuck his head out. Then the rest of his dandified person. His face was plastered with urbane politeness. He raised his eyebrows and smiled. "The return of the prodigal?" I noticed that one cuff hung loose, as though he had had his sleeves rolled. He was too fussy to have a button off. It would have been very easy for him to slip upstairs after assaulting me and before Clancy got in from the porch.

"The next time, Oglesbie, I'll stay away from draperies. No harm done, though, I can assure you. My head is stouter than you think."

He laughed indulgently. "You have been imbibing! I can't say that I blame you. As a matter of fact, I want to apol—"

"Skip it! I haven't the stomach for your patter now."

Lita annoyed me by explaining, "Paul had an accident. He isn't himself now."

"I quite understand." The smug monster bowed to her.

"I know damn well you do! And remember that I do too—now. Stick your monkey face back in and close the door. You irritate me!"

He complied after swallowing his smile. Lita said, "Paul, he was only trying to apologize for this afternoon. He knocked on the door and when I wouldn't answer he slipped a written apology under. I went downstairs when I heard you come in. Oglesbie couldn't have got past me—up or down. If there was anybody downstairs I didn't see him."

My head began to hurt again. Lita downstairs? I couldn't think. I pulled away from them and went for the cooling water in the bathroom. My head immersed, my fingers investigated the bump. It was sore as hell and so was I. Lita followed me, reading Oglesbie's note. "Do me the kindness to accept my apology, and permit me to explain. The person I mentioned is undoubtedly the one we should investigate. I have the details and will be most hap—"

"Shut it off! The bastard! The double-dyed, yellow . . ." I would have gone on indefinitely if Clancy hadn't insisted I be a gentleman. "That's enough, son! You get right to bed. You're not yourself and if you're not better by morning I'll call the doctor myself."

I heard him consoling Lita while I made awkward attempts to get undressed. The pounding and fog in my head. Then only the fog. . .

I was alone when I woke up. Something terrible had

happened but I couldn't remember. Lita was gone. And it was late morning with the sun beating in the room. Then Lita came through the door. Everything was all right again. She looked pale and had on the black dress.

She came over to me, sadness draping her. "How do you feel, Paul?"

"Not bad. Come closer." She kissed me but there was something gone from her. She had always been so sure, so young. She was no longer sure. I wanted to say something to bring it back to her but nothing came.

"I'll bring you coffee, Paul. Can you get up?"

"Sure." But I stayed on the bed. Every muscle was on strike. My head buzzed when I sat up to drink the coffee.

"She's here."

"Who?"

"Mrs. Selton."

I got up. Cold water against my skin brought some of the life back. A shave helped. Then I got dressed.

The corpse had come back.

CHAPTER SIXTEEN

WE COULD FEEL her presence as we sat stiffly in that up-stairs mourners' room. My head still ached but my senses were almost too receptive. The black-draped furniture with black-draped mourners, droopy white faces gloomy and moist, offended my sight. The aroma of moth balls sharpened that musty smell of aging bodies. The heavy odor of lilies and white lilacs from the rooms below. The discret murmur from those rooms, the faint rustle of old silk, the thought that she was there, holding her last soiree.

The heat. Phrases from Faulkner's "As I Lay Dying" danced through my brain. The stench of that fictional body filled my nostrils. Oglesbie was trying to get my attention. He had tried to talk to me earlier, putting his moist hand on mine, enraging me. He looked like a sick poodle, his eyes watering. Phillips was clean, sober, his hair slicked down with a wet comb.

We were all there—all the suspects. Lita, so sadly sweet that I wanted to bawl like a kid. Carol, her curves visible under the discreet black, biting her lips—wanting to cry but unable to. George hiding his discomfort with sullenness.

The chief mourners, Lovelace and Brundage. Brundage looking as though she might howl at any moment. The ancient people from the Hill, stiff, suspicious of us, curious, dry as dust, doing their duty to the name of Selton.

All was still downstairs. Lovelace got up. She removed a black cloth—disclosing her harp. Just as though we were at some weird recital of the damned, she picked the strings. The treacled melancholic strains flowed on the heat waves, loosening the tear ducts, bringing back the sobs from below. Brundage did howl, making her face hideous, flooding her handkerchief with more moisture than I thought she possessed. Phillips squirmed uncomfortably and I wanted to crawl under the sofa. Carol was twisting her handkerchief, letting the tears fall down to spot her dress. The old ladies from the Hill cried genteelly. The old men looked dispirited.

The music stopped. Lovelace took her place, and the minister took up from the drawing-room. He had a good speaking voice, so much so that I followed his inflections, losing the gist of his eulogy. Not so the mourners or Caroline, who felt that she belonged—they heard and were moved to more lamentation.

Then Lovelace picked "Nearer My God to Thee" from the taut strings while below the shuffle of feet over the thick carpet conveyed the knowledge that the corpse was being viewed! Lita's fingers pressing into my arm told me that she too was dreading the ordeal. The dead woman's friends were seeing to it that she was having the funeral she was entitled to, regardless of how she came by her death.

Then we were going down the steps to the emptied room. To the heavy scent of dying flowers, lifeless air, dead flesh and mortuary chemical. An aged patrician had Miss Lovelace on his arm. I watched her face as she looked down on the corpse. She must have been a very fine lady in her day—she had the manner. No hysteria, but sadness, regret. I saw her stiffen. Then a trembling that agitated the mound of veiling on her hat. She stood there while I craned my neck. Good God! No wonder she was startled. The eyes of the corpse were open!

Not wide open, but enough so that the glazed eyeballs were sinisterly visible. The mortician's art had failed— perhaps the heat or the official delay. At any rate, it was a shocking thing. Miss Lovelace had a black lace handkerchief to her face, and was sobbing loudly as her shaken partner propelled her forward.

Miss Brundage was kept from capsizing by her stout woman companion. She shrieked and threw herself about in a paroxysm of fear until she too was led away, to the arms of a chair and the dubious solace of smelling salts.

I whispered to Lita the cause of the disturbance. Carol had had no such preparation and suffered almost as much as Miss Brundage. George made a harsh exclamation in his throat and made way for us, carrying Carol from the distressing sight of her dead grandmother observing her and him.

Whether the heat had melted the wax or some other intricate device had gone suddenly wrong, the morticians had practiced their art to good effect. She lay there more composed than in real life, soft blackness draping her throat. But those eyes, as though she had opened them just to spy on us.

I looked back to watch Oglesbie. He stood there with Phillips coming up to join him. After one scared look, Phillips bolted for the porch, but Oglesbie seemed unable to move. His face took on the slack look that concentrated fear always gave him. An attendant took his arm and Oglesbie, his jaw trembling, fastened his vacant eyes on me.

I didn't move fast enough. He caught up with us and sat beside me going out to the cemetery. We had Phillips, too, and a strange man. In spite of the stranger's presence, Oglesbie kept up a rapid-fire of talk, which had little meaning except to express his fear. Phillips had his own memories which he was trying to keep down. He snarled at Oglesbie to shut his trap.

Fortunately the Mt. Auburn cemetery wasn't far. The

worst was over, the rest would be simple formality. And Mt. Auburn was a rest for fevered eyes. Lita and I had spent pleasant afternoons there among the old headstones, the rare shrubs and the view of ponds and hills. We had watched the Charles flowing past and looked across to Boston, hovered over Longfellow's grave and that of "grave Alice."

But we never thought we would be driving there back of the murdered Mrs. Selton, our eccentric landlady. And that we would be suspected of the murder. I looked across at Phillips. He was as dour as only a drinking man can be when he's forcing himself to stay sober.

We were there. Walking up the hill to the open grave. She had a beautiful site in which to rest—if that was any comfort. I noticed that everyone was very much affected when the closed coffin—could she still see through the cover?—was placed over the yawning hole. Then the lowering and the token scattering of dirt and the age-old words that have so much finality.

The flowers placed to hide the wound in the green grass. The uncontrolled sobbing now of Carol. Brundage making those queer animal sounds—couldn't she do anything with grace? Lovelace, lost in the past, reluctant to leave her old friend. She might feel better when the sod was placed neatly back and she and Brundage could bring flowers to place at the head.

We were going back. Mrs. Selton hadn't had her revenge yet, but convention demanded she be put under the ground.

She had presided at her last soiree. She couldn't or shouldn't come back to the Brattle Street house any more.

Phillips almost rushed up to his room. Poor fellow, his nerves must be shrieking. Oglesbie grabbed my arm, impervious to insult. "Redfern, please! I must see you." Lita walked on, leaving me with the creature. "You've got everything wrong, Redfern. You can cause me a great deal of trouble if you persist."

"That won't hurt my feelings."

"Now, really! Please listen! It was your seeing the picture of my wife that angered me. It wasn't your finding out about the hypnotism. I was just learning my 'power' then and I used her as a subject. I don't know why I ever took that snapshot—it's all I have now. She left me."

"What am I supposed to do—weep?" My head wasn't functioning any too well. "You got angry, Oglesbie, because the snapshot was positive proof that you could hypnotize people." But as I said it I knew that the reason he gave might also be genuine. Even he might have been capable of loving that girl.

I wanted to shake him, to discover more about the Stroke of Death. There would be something at Widener's. I knew I couldn't get any more out of him—he wanted me sidetracked to Phillips. He pushed his repulsive face close. "Phillips murdered his wife!" I jerked away but he followed. "I pieced that together from his ravings. She was too religious for him. It unsettled her mind. She belonged to the Mystic Yearners. Mrs. Selton backed that charlatanism until I extricated her. She had given this quack several thousand dollars."

"You didn't like that, did you, Oglesbie? You had to use your powers to induce her to save her money for a better purpose."

"You are correct. She clung to her superstitions stubbornly. It took a great many treatments to clear it out of her mind, even after I had proved that this man was using her money on women and liquor. She wouldn't let me have him prosecuted but she did withdraw her support."

He came even closer to whisper wetly in my ear, "Phillips must have found out. He came here with that knowledge and the remorse that has eaten at his soul, and strangled Mrs. Selton just as he hanged his wife."

He was willing that I pull away from him, so that he could enjoy my reception of his startling disclosure. I did look at him just as you look at a cockroach before stepping on it. "The main thing wrong with your story, Oglesbie, is that Phillips did not kill his wife. She hanged herself while he was out at sea—he found her there three weeks later, and cut her down."

I left him there, bathed in his own ill-spent sweat, and went upstairs. Lita had changed into a soft blue dress that made her look like an angel. She smiled as though we hadn't just come from a most distressing experience. "We're having some cold beer, Paul, green salad and sandwiches. All right?"

"Swell." It was easy to take her in my arms and kiss her.

"I'm going to the library right after lunch."

She stiffened in my arms. "Do you have to, Paul?"

"I have to." She didn't say any more and we ate our lunch. Carol came in just as we were finishing, George behind her. Carol didn't look any the worse for her emotional experience. It might have been because she was still up in the air. She refused our invitation to join us. "I came for the letters."

"My God, we told you we haven't got the letters!"

"You took them from me, Paul. Now I want them. There was a letter there announcing my birth. I may need it. George and I are going to get married."

I forgot to hide my surprise and the dark suspicion that followed—if she married George she wouldn't have to testify against him, in case there was something . . .

George read my thought. "We're getting married because we're in love and there's no sense putting it off. I'm not going to be inducted and leave Carol here. As soon as the Inspector lets us, we'll go home. She'll be safe there, and happy."

"Fine. Does the Inspector know you plan to marry so soon?"

"It is none of his business!" Carol snapped.

"Fine again. And I am sorry about the letters. Somebody took them. Who it was, I'm not sure yet. But I may know in a day or two."

Lita got up to congratulate George and to kiss Carol. She thought the idea was a splendid one and she didn't think they would question Carol. "You have grown so poised and self-reliant in the last weeks. But if they do, you can telegraph to Virginia." I wondered how Lita could be so sweet in the face of Carol's and George's boorish manners.

I hurried to the library as soon as they left. It seemed to me that I hadn't a moment to lose. The card catalog showed dozens and dozens of books on superstition. I had to search through a great many but finally I found it. In Southampton, England, about a century ago, people with goitre would pay a fee to the hangman to have their throats stroked by the bloody hand of the man who had just been hanged! There was a gruesome illustration of the hanging man, the severed hand, the people with swollen necks waiting—fearful but determined.

My previous knowledge was elaborately verified. I kept on reading the details. The last sentence stood out. I read it three times. It toppled over my case against Oglesbie.

"To be effective, the stroking had to be done in absolute silence."

It could have been done without hypnotism.

CHAPTER SEVENTEEN

I CLOSED the book, my thoughts going round and round. Absolute silence! Was that the reason we heard no sound? Could somebody who had knowledge of this superstition have induced Mrs. Selton to submit to a "cure"? It was possible. It would have to be somebody she had confidence in. Somebody who knew we had the ivory hand and palmed it off on Mrs. Selton as a dried human hand. Could she be that susceptible? I knew she could.

We had heard her begging Carol to stay with her that night. She expected something to happen. Lovelace said she was afraid of somebody. Brundage said she kept repeating, "Tonight! Tonight!" She was tense and quarrelsome, fear-ridden.

The Inspector could scoff at me but I knew I had something. The hypnotism angle might not be significant, but a hanged man's hand still pointed to the murderer.

I walked back home. Did Phillips know anything of this superstition? Against my will, the seed that Oglesbie had planted began to bear fruit. If it wasn't Oglesbie, it had to be somebody. He had spied on Phillips, probably gone through some old letters he had saved concerning his wife. He was wrong about Phillips murdering his wife, but that was an easy assumption from Phillips' ramblings. His conscience bothered him. She had made him feel guilty in spirit if not actually. But Phillips knew nothing of the ivory backscratcher unless he had found it on a table, a dresser. She might have been sitting with it in her hand. She was so gullible that on their first meeting while she stood in the garden, he might have mentioned that he knew a cure for her condition.

I had to find out whether Phillips had any previous knowledge of her. But first I had to know whether Mrs. Selton had been mixed up in this phony religion. I knocked on the old ladies' door. They might have both been dead for the response I got. But I had to know. I brought my kunckles sharply against the hard wood.

The door was opened by Lovelace. She certainly didn't look as though she had been sleeping. Her fine-drawn features were calm as she gave me an inquiring look. I kept my voice down, not wanting Oglesbie to hear me. "Did Mrs. Selton ever have anything to do with a religious group known as the Mystic Yearners?"

She stared at me before answering, "I don't know."

"But, Miss Lovelace, try to remember! It's terribly important to me."

Her scrutiny was like a cold hand, but my fever of anxiety didn't subside. She said, "Why?"

"Because I'm trying to solve her murder."

She accepted this. Her intelligent brow wrinkled in thought. "Everything has been so difficult that I'm afraid . . ."

Brundage crowded against her, pushing her disheveled face close to the well-groomed Lovelace. "What is it you want, young man?"

Lovelace, embarrassed, tried to squeeze her out of the aperture. Brundage had forgotten her teeth. Miss Lovelace said, "Amy! You're mushing your words." Amy put her hand in front of her mouth but refused to budge.

"I was asking Miss Lovelace if she knew anything about a phony religious group . . ."

"If you are referring to the Old South Church Third, young man!" she lisped indignantly.

I became patient. "No, I want to know about some psychic group that Mrs. Selton got mixed up in."

"Oh . . . !" She blinked her eyes and let her mouth fall inward. Then her eyes snapped and her lips worked, "I recall! Mystic . . . Mystic . . ."

Lovelace pulled her back. "Amy, you're thinking of the river."

"I am not! There was a terrible man that she was giving money to. We had no idea. Carrie would slip out . . . Why, this man was a . . ."

Lovelace was losing patience. "Amy!"

Before the door was closed in my face I pleaded, "Can't you remember his name? Or where he is? Or was?"

"Kraski? Kerlaski? Krobansky? . . ." In a way I didn't blame Lovelace for closing the door. Amy had never sounded so witless. I had to guess at the sounds she was making, her lips too loose, her cheeks like sagged sails. Lovelace's pride couldn't put up with the spectacle.

I knocked at Phillips' door. He grunted, "Come in," and stiffly swung his feet off the bed. He was very drunk and belligerent. I would have to go easy. "Nice day, isn't it?"

"Is it?" He was in an ugly mood. He reached clumsily for the bottle, gurgled a stiff gulp and wiped his mouth with the back of his hand. The red streak was still angry and unhealed! "She was dead but she looked at me!"

His conscience was as disturbed as the scar on his hand as his bloodshot eyes looked through me. I kept my voice smooth, undisturbing. "Your wife knew her."

"Yes, she took me past here once . . . said that was the way we'd have it if I got religion . . ." I felt my heart swelling up, suffocating me. *He had a reason for murdering Mrs. Selton!* His remorse over his wife's suicide goading him, steeping him in jealous rage, driving him against this rich old woman who had everything, the power to build a cult that filled his wife with hope and then despair. That made her nag at him in life and now more in death.

I forgot to go easy. "You came here to kill the old lady."

His hate was as sudden and as cold-blooded as a rattlesnake's. Before I could move, he sprang toward me and sent his scarred fist crashing against my face. "You damned stool pigeon! You dirty yellow mouthpiece!"

Blood was streaming from my nose, the hot sweetish taste of it in my mouth, as I sent my fist into his granite face. He was cursing me, moving in, closer, giving me two blows for one, the blood on his fists mine now, not his—has face a cold mask of efficiency, insensible to my taps.

One of his sledge-hammers sent sparks from my eyes before they closed, the other crumpled me inward at the pit of my stomach. There was no kindly referee, but heavy boots pitched me like a leaky grain sack into the middle of the hall. The door slammed.

I couldn't see from my blood-smeared face. I got up with difficulty and, having a nice sense of direction, opened my own door. Lita screamed. It hurt my ears. "Don't, Lita. Show me where you keep the bathroom."

It wasn't easy listening to her sobs, hearing her pleas to keep out of trouble, feeling her hands on my face as she wiped away the gore. Striving to recapture some of my self-respect. "Get out, Lita, please. I'll finish up."

Gallons of cold water gave my eyes the courage to open. What I saw wasn't much. My nose seemed off-base and was swollen like an over-ripe persimmon. My mouth looked as though I'd met a swarm of wasps head-on.

Lita was angry when I put on my gardening pants and an old shirt. Still angrier when I sat with the door ajar, watching for Phillips to come out. But I was mad, clean through, and I meant to sit there. Phillips must have taken a nap after his exertions, slight as they were. He didn't come out for a long time.

When he did, I stole down the stairs after him, oblivious to Lita's stony disapproval and her worry over the writs summoning us to appear before the judge on the following Monday. It gave me a jolt just as it did Lita—it was so damned official-looking, so sure! Justice blindfolded, with the scales that never quite balanced. But if they were going to turn somebody over to the Grand Jury I meant to see that that somebody was the right one. And there wasn't much time.

Phillips got into a taxi a block down on Brattle. I was waving another one down when Clancy grabbed my arm. "Sure, and I didn't know you, Paul." He pulled back. "Say, man! You've been in a mixup."

"Yes, Clancy, but I can't stop now." I shouted to the driver to keep the other cab in sight. Clancy was giving me a stern fatherly look. His big voice boomed as I was being carried away, "I won't be there night times after this. Take care . . ."

Poor Clancy! The Inspector was putting somebody in who could keep a closer watch on us—somebody who wouldn't be afraid of ghosts. I wondered if the ghost knew.

Clancy looked happier—it was better for him to be out of that house at night so long as he didn't lose his job.

I blinked my eyes in the bright sunshine that still held the street, flashed sharply on the Charles. They ached. First my head bashed in and now my face beaten out of shape. I'd be lucky if I got out of this thing alive. And Lita, back in those rooms, the walls closing in on her. Not wanting me to do anything, but fearful.

I cursed the cabby when he lost the grey cab across the river. Following one with a pretty girl alone on the back seat. Spurred by my expletives, he slid close to two other grey cabs. "That's the one!" My arteries knew even before I recognized the slumped figure, so inert and yet capable of murderous ferocity.

We swung into Scollay Square behind him, pulled ahead when his cab stopped. I saw him get out, toss a bill to the driver and go into a honky tonk bar. I paid off and propped myself against the side of the building. The vivid movement of the street hurt my eyes, the raucous sounds my ears, the smells were fiercely noisome. Rotting fruit, rancid popcorn oil, greasy meat, old clothes, decaying wood, people sweating.

It was hard to keep from sliding down, closing my eyes. My body ached in every bone. A sailor grinned sheepishly at me when a ragged boy shoved a snapshot before him. "Want to buy my sister? Want to buy my sister?" Juke baxes blaring. Sickening scent from a barber shop. Was the old goat going to stay in there all day?

He came out finally, weaving a minute to get his bear-
ings, went down the street, hesitated, and went into
another bar. I knew that I might as well go home. I was a
sick man. I could take what little knowledge I had to
the Inspector. At the thought of his sneers, my back
stiffened. The time seemed endless. Sailors, soldiers, sea-
men, shoddy girls, shifty-eyed civilians, all passed and
re-passed like a stream of ants on the loose.

My eyes closed against the glare. I almost missed Phillips.
He was going down the street. This time he seemed to
know where he was going. He stopped in front of a tattoo
parlor and my heart sank. Was I going to have to stand
through that?

Before I could lean against the building, he slipped into
the shop next door. I eased myself over. My heart did a
dull tattoo as I read the fulsome sign, "Kalski—Psychic,
Palmist, Mystic, Astrologer, Occult Diviner, Religious
Seer. Bring your troubles. Get the answer. Special rates
to all those in Service."

Could this be the Kraski, Kerlaski, Krobansky, of Amy's
muddled speech? And the one that Phillips knew through
his wife? I wanted to believe. It was like reaching up
through murky water to a straw that looked like a plank.
Sleazy drab curtains hid the windows.

Was Phillips going in to strangle the man with his bare
hands? Would he come out soon and walk casually down
the street, his work done? Methodically trying to lay the
ghost of his wife, so he could ship out again—nobody,

least of all the Inspector, suspecting? Who would pay attention to Oglesbie—or to me for that matter?

Voices—I could hear a mumble when I stood close to the door. Then silence. No outcry as yet. The voices again, dull, monotonous, reiterative. More silence—drawn out.

Then Phillips stood in front of me. His arms hung loose. Fear filled my belly as the mean eyes brooded into mine. I brought meanness into my own. He wouldn't catch me off-guard this time. This time it would be different! I'd probably be run over by two trucks in Scollay —after being kicked into the street.

"I can't ship out!" He wasn't even seeing me. He recognized my face. He should! He made it what it was. But his mind was boring inward—on himself. "Ain't that a hell of a note, Mac? They'll get me next time. My number's up. On account of me the whole ship will be blown to hell!"

My puny muscles relaxed. "Don't believe that guff. They have to say something. That fakir . . ."

"It's in my hand." The broad palm trembled as he traced the life line. "It's in my head." He clumsily felt the bumps that were put there by better men than I. "I'll never see land again."

I got sore. "You're crazy, Phillips! Quit mumbling that junk. Is this the man . . ."

"The stars too. No matter how we zig-zag, the tin fish . . . Like rats in a trap . . ."

Some light seeped into the dark place I call my mind.

"Phillips! If that's his line he may be something besides a quack. He may be an enemy agent."

He wasn't following me. He was still seeing himself drowned. "You've never seen one of those things sliding your way, Mac. I can't do it! And I can't do anything else."

"Listen, Phillips, for God's sake quit whining. He can't foretell the future any more than I can." He was ambling up the street with me after him.

He turned. "This one knows. He predicted the old lady's murder. She laughed at him and in two hours she was dead."

"What old lady?" I couldn't feel anything, just a numbness.

He turned around to where I was standing, frowning at my stupidity. "The old lady! The one in the house!"

I grabbed his arm. "You don't mean Mrs. Selton? Why, how did he see her?"

He jerked away. Walked on. "He was up there. She wrote him a letter. When he says somebody is going to die—they die."

I caught him just before he stepped into a spa. "Phillips, listen, did this Kalski tell you that he was there talking to her just two hours before her murder?"

"Let go of me! Didn't I just tell you? And he said I was going to die . . . drown like a rat down there . . ." He disappeared into the dark interior, his voice drowned as his woes soon would be.

So Kalski had been there with her. He was the one she had been quarreling with. He had gone there to blackmail . . . ?

I had to see Kalski.

CHAPTER EIGHTEEN

I WALKED back and stood in front of the tattoo shop while I gathered my few wits. Then I walked in.

He was a big man, flabby as a dead clam. Sparse sandy hair and eyes, pale without expression. He could see out of them but nobody could see in. "You want a reading?"

"Give me the works."

He held out his hand. "Five dollars." I tried to put the bills on the palm without touching the clammy flabbiness.

"You don't work." My flesh crawled as he held my hand.

"I'm going out in the Merchant Marine. Want to do my bit."

My eyes kept wandering about. Dirt. Clutter. Disgusting smell. Another room in the back, limp curtains not hiding the sagging bed, the small window high at the foot of the bed. Did he really have a letter from Mrs. Selton? I looked at the table by the outside door—some letters there. More papers, newspaper clippings on a stand in the back room.

"I am afraid you will have to give me your attention." There was menace in his voice. He might have had a time with Phillips, before he scared hell out of him. Phillips probably came there for trouble and not his fortune.

I grinned sheepishly. "Never been in one of these places before. Want to know what's going to happen to me before I go out."

He settled to his work. Something in my hand—he shook his head as though reluctant to disclose it. Checked up on my head, his fingers making my scalp crawl. I had a chance to stare around. A skull and cross bones on a dusty shelf. A pickled tarantula. Some Indian relics.

He was standing in front of me now, staring sadly down from his six feet four. He told me a lot of cut and dried stuff, fifty per cent right. I nodded in complete agreement. He settled into the chair, spoke unctuously. "You love your wife. You love your little children. If you go to sea you will never see them again. It's all there, in your hand, your head. Now I will go into my trance and consult the occult. Give me your hand to establish communion."

My eyes were free to wander around while he did his mumbo-jumbo. It was true—his line was instilling fear when he couldn't actually keep men from serving their country. One way was almost as bad as the other. Boston wasn't Cambridge, but the Inspector would have to see that he was investigated on that score. The departments in the two cities must have to work together often.

The man must have blood like a fish, his hand was so clammy on a hot day. If I could only grab that bunch of letters as I went out. My eyes went back again to the shelf. What an assortment of gruesome objects! Probably did a lucrative "healing" business on the side. A head, brown skin, gaping mouth, coarse black hair.

I jerked convulsively in my chair. He spoke sharply. I sat very still then. The head was a human head, shrunk to the size of a grapefruit! And from the neck hung a hand—a shrunken human hand, like the bleached claw of a bird. A dirty piece of paper was curled up on the hand. I knew. I knew without being able to read it that the paper bore the legend, "The Stroke of Death."

I must have looked awed enough to suit him when he opened his eyes, "I repeat, 'Don't go to sea. Stay away from munitions. Let them put you in a camp. You have a right to life. To love.'"

I stumbled to my feet, thanking him, "I won't go. I won't." I tried to scurry over to the door before he got up. But he was more agile than I thought. His eyes were like a lizard's now, with the sun on them.

I bumped against the table, still watching him. My arm shot up, my fingers closed on the stiff hair, and I scurried out the door, the gruesome head and dangling hand clutched tightly. I heard his scream of rage as the sunshine of Scollay hurt my eyes. Felt his fat fingers on my back, heard my shirt tear as I wrenched loose and sprinted up the street.

In and out among the apathetic crowd, thanking God that anything could happen in Scollay and nobody would care. Only Kalski, and he might send a knife burying itself in my bare back where the torn shirt flapped. I ran, my nerves tingling with the feel of the black hair, the thought of the hideous thing I held.

I ducked into the first drug store and into a phone booth. The light went on when I closed the door. The head was even more monstrous now that the dust had fallen off. The mouth open, as though the creature had died in agony, the repulsive luxuriance of hair, weighting the head, pushing the grisly features forward. It was something that should be decently buried, not put upon a shelf.

I read the paper, the illegible scrawl, "The Stroke of Death." A face loomed up at the glass door. Blurry. Could it be Kalski? My eyes focused and the blood quit pounding in my temples. It wasn't Kalski—it was a stranger.

He was staring at me, horror and curiosity in his face. My God! I'd have to get out of there or somebody'd turn me in as a maniac. I stepped out of the booth, trying to pretend that holding a dried human head with severed hand attached was the most ordinary thing in the world. I looked furtively about for Kalski. He wasn't there. The

stranger I ignored, in spite of his scrutiny and his edging
away from me.

The girl at the counter was watching me. I stepped
over. She looked kind. "Can you give me a sack to put
this in?" She screamed when I held it up, so I had to fade
out of the door. How in God's name was I going to get
the thing over to the Inspector?

A taxi, of course. I stopped one, some instinct driving
my hand to my pocket. No money—small change. I appealed to him, "Listen, if you'll take me to the Cambridge
Police Station and then home to Brattle, I'll pay you then."
I should have kept my mouth shut—a good look at me
and the thing I held and he scooted off.

There was nothing for it but the subway. As people
stared at me and gave me a wide berth, I stuck the damn
thing into the front of my shirt. The pinched features
pressed into my skin, making me sick at the stomach.
The hand crawled around with the lurchings of the train.

I kept telling myself: It's nothing. It's not alive. Been
dead for ages. At one time it probably slunk through the
South American jungles. Somebody caught it and killed
it. Sure they killed it first. Then they removed part or all
of the skull and shrunk it with live steam. I felt myself
turning green.

And it was only Park. I had to change for Central.
Pressed in with the home-going crowd, I tried to keep
my stomach down where it belonged. I thought of Lita.
Lita in one of her dances. Suddenly I looked down at the

woman sitting in front of me. She was staring at my waistline, her eyes dilated. She was a sharp, bright-looking person, not at all the soft hysterical type. She probably thought I was a pretty rum-looking individual. My eyes followed hers. The claw-like hand was dangling down!

I pulled it back against my skin and squeezed closer to the entrance. Whew! The train stopped and I hurried up into the square. I almost ran to the Cambridge Station, past the painted likeness of John J. McBride and up the stairs to the Inspection Division.

Inspector Green was in. He would see me. This time I had something to show him. He looked—looked at the shrivelled head and claw hand—then looked at me. He wasn't impressed. Behind his blandness, he was laughing at me. Even after I explained Kalski.

"You do believe this is important, don't you? This is The Stroke of Death. Kalski knew about it as well as Oglesbie. He told Phillips he was there just before the murder. He was undoubtedly the one she was quarreling with. As I told you, Phillips knew of Mrs. Selton. He had a grudge against her. Kalski knew of her. He also had a grudge . . ."

"And so did a great many other people."

I felt sick. Not actively as when I had the odious trophy that now sat on the Inspector's desk, but dead sick.

I watched his long fingers playing with an envelope that he had picked from among other labelled envelopes in a drawer. I wanted to say more to convince him that I wasn't just a fool, but I had gone dead all over.

He put down a white sheet of paper as though he were preparing a parlor trick, and slid something from the envelope onto the sheet. My nerves tightened long before my brain got the message. My eyes saw the thing on the white paper—the blue stone twinkling in the gold mounting—just one of Lita's earrings.

My nerves leaped as the message struck. I felt the pulse in my temple throbbing . . . He had the other earring—he had always had the other earring—since the night of the murder. When I raised my eyes to meet his there was almost a touch of sympathy in his . . .

His voice was cold. "You picked up the other earring from under the chair where she was strangled. You did not know that she *kept* this one for us—hugged tight between her breasts, where it lodged . . ."

"It's a damn lie! Lita didn't do it! She couldn't do it!"

I fell into a chair, my hands tight against my face. Men don't blubber or sob or cry. They make hideous sounds of choking, stabbing at the fear that rises like a poison gas from the weeds, the grass, everything! I freed my face, stood in front of him. "You're a devil! You're a damn dirty devil! You'll never fasten this on Lita. Never!"

I went out of there, leaving him with his smile.

CHAPTER NINETEEN

WHEN I OPENED my eyes the next morning Lita was smiling down at me. She looked so pretty, leaning on her elbow, her nightie fallen from one shoulder, that I smiled back. It came to me right away—about the earring. But I didn't remember how I got home or what I said.

"Do you feel better?" Her voice was like a warm chinook. "You were so tired last night that you fell right on the bed and fell asleep. I had a hard time getting your clothes off."

"Did you think I was loopy?"

"Of course not. I knew you were dead tired."

And I knew I was too. I knew that I couldn't move. Lita said, "Feel like going to a wedding this morning?"

"I don't mind." But I did mind. I didn't want to do anything. Two hours later Lita and I were standing back of George and Carol, witnessing their marriage. Every-thing seemed to be in order and I asked no questions. I felt as pallid as a convalescent.

When we got back to the house, Lovelace met us at the door. She looked shocked when Carol told her but recov-ered almost instantly and warmly congratulated George and wished Carol happiness in South Dakota.

"Mr. Platts, your grandmother's lawyer, is here, Caro-line. You might like to know what disposition your grandmother made of her property. He is going to read the will."

I perked up then. The will? Somebody must be pretty anxious. Miss Lovelace answered my raised eyebrow. "Dr. Oglesbie got permission from the Inspector." Better and better. I found myself grinning—it made my face hurt.

Mr. Platts was standing with his back to the fireplace, looking beyond and above his rapt audience, the legal paper in his hand not daring to crackle. He was everything that a Cambridge lawyer should be, like a sturdy volume on a shelf that discreetly hid its contents behind the one word, "Platts."

The good doctor, his lips moist with anticipation, sat where he could get a full view of the others. Brundage, blinking her eyes, irritated at the delay, was next in the semicircle. Then Lita, happy when she looked at George and Carol on the love-seat, but not happy enough to clear the deep well of worry in her lovely eyes. I chose to stand on the bottom step of the hall stairs—too nervous to sit still. Lovelace dropped gracefully into the only chair left in view—the death chair.

I was thinking how quickly horror fades from our minds. These friends of Mrs. Selton's anxious to gobble up her earthly goods. Lita, so anxious to right all wrongs and make people happy.

I hadn't been listening. ". . . Payment of my just debts (of which I am sure there are none)," Mr. Platts coughed apologetically and continued in his safe voice, "and funeral expenses and the amounts which may be assessed and payable as inheritance or excise taxes, I give, devise and bequeath as follows: First—To my good friend and advisor, Dr. Frederick Oglesbie, the sum of $50,000 so that he may be free to finish his great book."

There was a screech from Brundage. Her face worked as though she were being boiled in oil. Her hands shot out in appeal to Lovelace, whose face I couldn't see, "We saw the will. That wasn't in it. This is a forgery!" She rushed on Oglesbie, whose moist lips were spread in a wide smile. It looked as though there was going to be another murder. "You did this! You went up and got the real will that first night. You . . . !" She was pulling at his Van Dyke, Oglesbie's small hands up trying to protect himself.

Mr. Platts intoned, "This will is in order. Mrs. Selton came to my office on March thirteenth and had this new will drawn up. She was of sound mind and it is entirely in order. May we proceed?"

It might have been funny if murder weren't involved.

Brundage had resumed her seat, her sobs and disjointed phrases filling the room. "She went back on her word . . . You could never trust Carrie . . . I never mentioned my own niece except for the usual dollar . . ."

"Shall we continue?" Mr. Platts was raising his voice.

Dr. Oglesbie said, "Pray do," his peculiar sense of humor manifesting itself. I wouldn't have been surprised to see him thumb his nose at Brundage. The good doctor had fixed things for himself. His "power" was earning him dividends.

"Second—The rest, residue and remainder of my property, real, personal and mixed, and wherever situated, I leave, to be divided in equal shares, to (a) Miss Evelyn Lovelace; (b) Miss Amy Brundage."

Brundage snapped, "How much is left after throwing away $50,000?"

"The estate is in excess of $250,000." A startled whistle escaped me at this pronouncement. $250,000? Who would have thought it? Dr. Oglesbie said teasingly, "You see, ladies, there is plenty for all of us. We shouldn't quarrel. We shall be able to live in peace and comfort . . ."

"You can live where you like," Brundage warned, "but you shan't live here! And you can take your skulls with you!"

Suddenly I knew as I looked at them which one had committed the murders, both of Mrs. Selton and the cat. I had had suspicions before, now I was sure. As sure as I was standing there! The shock of certainty set my nerves quivering. Then I felt depressed. Horribly depressed. One of those people—it couldn't be true—had twisted the scarf . . .

George and Carol were sitting there like kids at a movie; neither one concerned that this large estate that really belonged to Carol was not to be theirs. Lovelace got up. She nodded to Oglesbie. "I am glad she remembered you." She turned to the lawyer. "If that is all, Mr. Platts?"

"There is something more." He seemed embarrassed, like a prompter shoved forward in the star's role. He swallowed discreetly, "There is a codicil."

We all stared at him. Oglesbie sitting upright, Lovelace rooted to the faded Oriental. We heard, after the inevitable throat-clearing, "In case my daughter, Mrs. Evelyn Selton Barrie, or her children, or her children's children, should get in touch with me before my death, I leave one dollar to the above three good friends, Miss Evelyn Lovelace, Miss Amy Brundage, and Dr. Frederick Oglesbie. The rest, residue and remainder of my property, real, personal and mixed, and wherever sit—"

He got no further before the storm broke. Brundage was on her feet. "That isn't legal! That's nonsense! That's . . ." Oglesbie was wiping his hands—the room seemed suddenly very hot to him. "Are you sure that codicil is in order? Is it possible to change the whole context of the will by adding . . ."

"I am afraid it is. She came to me a few days after making this last will. We had three witnesses. She knew what she was doing. She still had hope that her beloved daughter or her offspring would relent enough to come to her. The cards kept telling her that she would get her wish."

Carol sobbed, "Poor Grandma! If we'd only known before!"

Brundage shook an already shaking finger at her. "You knew it! You found it out—that's the reason you came. She didn't love you . . ." Oglesbie said nothing further. He slumped back in his chair, his hopes unrealized. Carol had stopped crying. "Do you mean, Mr. Platts, that this house and the money is all ours?"

"It is all yours—with the exception of the three dollars."

Carol got up, pulled George to his feet beside her. "We're rich, George!" He looked dazed, a sickly grin overspreading his irregular features. Lita was beaming. She shook hands with Carol. "I'm so happy for you, Carol! It's come out right. It had to! All those years that your mother and your grandmother suffered . . ."

As though remembering something, Carol turned suddenly to Dr. Oglesbie. "I want those letters."

His smile started out as a sneer. "My dear girl, I want you to have them, but don't look at me."

"Well, somebody in this room took them and I . . ."

I signalled to Lita. There was nothing to be gained listening to Carol harp on her letters. I knew where they were. But there was another letter more important—that was the letter that Kalski had. I had to get it. The Inspector might try and then again he might not think it important. It had to be done soon to keep another murder from happening in that house!

Lita was making her way past Oglesbie, sympathy in her face. Past Brundage who was on the verge of a stroke. Even more sympathy for her. She hesitated before Lovelace, wondering what to say to bring the life back to that face. Before she could utter the words, Brundage took command of the situation. "Come, Evelyn! We'll go up to our rooms. I have never heard of anything so criminal!" She stopped before Lovelace, who had undergone a pathetic shrinkage. "You have nothing to worry about. I will always take care of you."

My mouth dropped open as Lovelace meekly followed her. That was the first time we had ever seen Evelyn follow in the backwash of anyone, least of all Brundage. I looked over at Oglesbie—he was the pulpiest, sickliest-looking person I had ever seen. All his work on Mrs. Selton, and it came to this!

We were in our own rooms. I locked the door. "We may as well start going through our junk."

"Move, Paul?" She looked suddenly tired. "I don't know where to begin, but I'm glad to go."

I looked away, made myself get busy. When Lita was going through some stuff in the bedroom, I slipped out, locked the door after me and went down the back way into the garden. It took a bit of digging around to find the earring after I got the back-scratcher handle. Lita was

still busy when I got upstairs. I took the gloves out of
their hiding place, put the three things in an envelope.
The Inspector might as well have everything now—there
was no use holding anything back from him. On a slip of
paper I wrote a name and after that—"The one who knew
—without seeing or—" Damn it, what was the use putting anything more—I would have to prove it!

He wasn't there when I got to the Division, so I left it
on his desk. They told me there were no new develop-
ments.

That night I told Lita that I would have to break into
Kalski's place. She pleaded with me, but I told her there
was no other way. I had to frighten her to make her promise to keep the door bolted and under no circumstances
to open it. She had heard me earlier in the evening insist-
ing that George and Carol leave the house—go to a hotel.
This was their honeymoon—nothing must happen to anyone.

Out in the hall, the black shadows crept up, pressing
against my eyeballs, as I felt along the wall. Voices—
low, unhurried, frightening. Phillips, going through his
particular hell. Any minute I knew I might be plugged.
Or slugged by Mrs. Selton's ghost. My feet easing down
. . . how many more steps? Clancy gone. A more alert
man . . . men outside.

My heart beating loud enough to wake the dead as I
leaned against a pillar on the back porch. No moon. Just
stars, remote Cambridge stars. Creeping from shrub to

shrub, my back vulnerable. Through a hole in the hedge. Careless, easy walk past a dick, then a cab.

Scollay, crawling with night life. Rats, human and beast. Jolly drunks. Sodden ones. The alley back of Kalski's. My dimout flash showed an old warehouse. The door creaked when I opened it. I waited, shivering in spite of myself, downing the fear that is as old as man—fear of the dark, the unknown, the furtive things that met my feet, stopped dead, then scurried. I could imagine their beady eyes. I turned on the purplish light—a slim finger outlining the crates, the piles of dirt and rubbish. The smell was putrid.

I was making my way to Kalski's window. It was open —my light picked up the sullen movement of dirty curtain. I was thinking of Lita waiting at our window, worrying. The thought sent my feet faster. I clumsily kicked something soft that moved. A sepulchral groan lifted, filled the old warehouse, freezing me.

Blood flowing back into the arteries, I could look at the body—not dead or gory—just a drunk. I moved ahead, my bruised body protesting as I hoisted myself to the window ledge. I almost fell back again when my light showed Kalski spread out almost below me. I could have sworn that his eyes were open, watching me, waiting. No, they were closed. Naked on the bed, the man was enormous— a vast inert mass, lardy, repulsive.

I felt like a mountain cat as I eased my body through the opening and to a chair, then to the floor. My ears were alert—I hadn't made a sound. Straight to the letters. My first impulse was to stuff them all in my pocket and get out. No, I must be sure. Only one that wasn't a bill. And it wasn't the right one.

Muted shouts down the square as I turned the flash on other parts of the room. Steps going by—must keep the flash down. Kalski could shoot me as an intruder. A cop could shoot me if I started to run from Kalski. I went stealthily to another table. Opened a box—broken spectacles, a couple of teeth, yellow, horrible roots. I closed the box. Where the devil had he put the letter? Had he destroyed it—it would have been the smart thing to do. I opened a well-thumbed Bible—using the Book for his own nefarious ends!

The pages jerked past as I held the flash in one hand. An envelope fell forward. My heart pounded in a dull rhythm as I recognized the handwriting. We had received notes in that script, crabbed, painstaking rounded letters. I felt like shouting. Instead I placed the letter inside my shirt and moved carefully to the front door. My errand had been successful—I was a pretty good detective. A cab and then home to Lita.

The key turned easily. My hand on the knob, a stinging pain pierced my shoulder, travelled down my arm. A thick voice, "Turn around!"

I faced Kalski. He jabbed the knife in front of my heart. I felt the trickle of blood running down my skin as the knife bit in—only a touch but enough pain to jar the whole nervous system. His eyes were alive now as I stared at him, strange, pale eyes, filled to the brims with some peculiar kind of hatred. "Before I push this in, why did you come back?"

There was no use lying to him. Lita was right—I shouldn't have tried to play detective. "You knew Mrs. Selton. You went to see her the night she was murdered."

The knife bit in as he tightened his grip. "Yes, I was there. She told me to come. Then the old bitch denied it. She was crazy—nutty as a fruit cake."

My back was braced against the door—my muscles stiff against the cut of the knife. Down the street I could hear men singing—a lusty song of life. There was no use appealing to him. He was the sort who likes to kill when he can get away with it. "If you kill me, you'll be dragged in for the murder. The Cambridge police know you were at the scene of the crime, that you quarrelled with Mrs. Selton, that you knew of 'The Stroke of Death.' I gave them the head and withered hand . . ."

As fear possessed him, his hand wavered. In that moment I hit the knife a sharp blow, sending it scraping across my skin to clatter against the table. Before he could grab it, I sent my fist into the side of his head. He cursed and came back at me, slugging me a heavy one in the pit of the stomach.

The blow was so deadly that I started to crumple. Kalski was on the floor on one knee, his guard up, the other hand reaching for the knife. If he got that knife, I would be dead in a flash. The pain of its scrape was still searing me. In a flash, I was on him, yelling Indian-fashion at the top of my lungs, fighting for my life.

He had the knife—I saw the flash of it from the street light through the glass-topped door. He was slowly turning in spite of my blows—his strength so much greater. I didn't want to die there in that filthy hole—leaving Lita to face—

My yells had brought us an audience. Shadows moved outside the door—laughter—shouts of encouragement. Then silence as they moved on to a better show. The knife was raised.

I jerked my body loose as he raised himself to strike. My arm grasped the rickety table and I sent it crashing down on his head. The top broke off, leaving the legs in my hand. The knife was still in his hand and he was laughing spasmodically, blowing like a fish, sending a stench from his sweaty nakedness.

I wasn't yelling—it had become hard to breathe even as my eyes stayed fascinated on the glint of the knife, my body bending and twisting. I had to jump as he lunged at me. Close to the door, I sent the table legs crashing through the glass.

There was that second when I stood, the sound of splintering glass in my ears, a perfect target. My head bobbed down just as the knife cut through my hair. The sound and feel of it infuriated me. I pounced on him, furious enough to tear him limb from limb. I had the lust to crush out every bit of life in his hated body.

He was crushing me when something hit me on the head.

When I came to I was in the Joy Street Police Station, not the least bit joyful. I came to fighting—until I saw the uniform and a night stick descending . . . My hands flew to my battered head. "Please! I'm all right now. Get Inspector Green of the Cambridge Division. Tell him Kalski's here." I looked over at Kalski, looking the worse for wear, draped in one of his filthy curtains. He didn't look funny to me. I yelled, "He's an enemy agent! Don't let him go. He's mixed up in the Selton murder. The Inspector will tell you I was gathering evidence . . ."

Along with Kalski and some drunken bums who gave us a wide berth, I was ignominiously herded out the door. We were placed in cells in the new courthouse. The bum in my cell, after a disgusted look at me, went to sleep on one of the cots. I paced the floor, aching in every bone, my head a mass of confusion and pain. Across my body was a crusted line of blood. What would Lita think? What was she thinking now? She would think I was dead. And I damn near was.

CHAPTER TWENTY

THE LETTER? I kept thinking of the letter as I paced. It wasn't in my shirt—the shirt was almost torn off my back. My pockets were cleaned—not even a cigarette— police ritual. Maybe they had picked up the letter. My glass breaking must have brought them on the run. Good thing they banged me over the head—Kalski would have finished me with the knife after having fun with his fists.

The dawn was beginning to break, etching the barred window on the unyielding wall, when I turned suddenly to see Lita standing, looking in. She drew back when she saw me. I must have been a pretty sight. "Lita!"

"Yes, Paul." The throaty voice. The features lighting up, moving closer when she recognized me. Her eyes were violet-shadowed but she was loveliness itself in a lilac cotton. I couldn't take my eyes from her.

I hadn't heard Inspector Green or seen him. "Do you want to get out or not? You've given me enough trouble! But the boys at Joy Street said I could have you and welcome." He motioned to a guard who unlocked the door. I was free. I was afraid to kiss Lita—I might be crawling with lice—I knew I was dirty and bloody. But I took her hands and pressed them.

The sun's glow was seeping into the sacrosanct courthouse when we left it. The Inspector handed me a sealed envelope when he motioned us into his car. I tore it open, unmindful of his sarcastic reference to "valuables." "The letter—it isn't here."

"No." Then he decided to loosen up, "I have it. Your wife got me up. Made me go with her down to Kalski's place. Fortunately I knew where it was. We were going to move in ourselves—but you always have to do the dramatic."

"When were you going to move in?" I challenged.

"In a day or so. I was following some other leads—the little package you left."

"A day or so wasn't soon enough for us. Monday isn't far off. Besides there's more murder coming unless you move fast."

"It is unfortunate that you are not a member of our Division." He was driving across the Charles, on which the sun glinted, gilding the sails of a small boat. And our wonderful vacation almost gone. I spoke bitterly. "Being a suspect makes one move fast."

We were going up Brattle. The Inspector volunteered, "You were right about Kalski. We found the evidence—he is in enemy pay. He's small fry, but maybe we can get him to talk. We have the murder to hold over his head. As a matter of fact, Redfern, you haven't done too badly."

"Thank you for your enthusiasm."

"You're entirely welcome. Now take a bath and get some sleep." The car had stopped in front of the house. The old chilblain even smiled, not too frostily, at Lita as he let us out. She started up the path. I said to the Inspector, "How about the gloves?"

His eyes shrouded. "Report not in yet."

I remembered to thank him for getting me out. He hadn't mentioned the earring on the ivory handle—he wouldn't. But he would know . . .

A piercing scream shut off my thoughts. It was Lita. I was up the path like a streak, looking past her through the door. Oglesbie was standing, white-faced, wiping his hands. Phillips was coming down the stairs, shambling, bewildered. And in the death chair was a figure, a blood-red scarf dangling . . .

I walked in slowly and looked at the figure. Lovelace! The scarf was tied around her throat! Oglesbie was gibbering, "I didn't do it! I didn't do it!" He pointed to Phillips. "He must have done it. I heard him moving around and muttering all night." Phillips was swearing, making for Oglesbie.

The corpse groaned. I looked closer, then at the Inspector, who had followed me. Then down at Lovelace, who was making pitiful sounds now, her lovely hands beating the air. The tongue was out. It wasn't congested —only slightly. But she looked horrible, her eyes bugging out, clawing . . .

I reached around and loosened the scarf with one yank. Whoever had tied the scarf hadn't intended that she die— too fast. Once freed of it, she crumpled forward.

Then I remembered poor Brundage. What a fool I had been not to think of her sooner. She must have been strangled too, and before . . . I dashed up the stairs, calling back, "Look after her, Lita. Come with me, Inspector!"

The door was locked. We hurled our strength against it. Damn the doors! They were as solid as iron. The Inspector picked up the iron cat and hurled it at the door. It took several blows before the lock sprung for us, and we could enter.

Brundage was there, in the inner room, face turned, an orange scarf knotted about her neck. The same indelible marks that Mrs. Selton's face had borne. The tongue sticking out, thick with blood inside. Purple splotches on her cheeks. The eyes . . . My God! I turned away sickened at the sight. There was no doubt that she was dead and had been for some time.

The Inspector's face was hard—hard as the stone cat we kicked aside on our way downstairs. He made some calls while I answered Lita's questioning eyes. Quick tears filled hers as she bent to administer to Miss Lovelace, propped up in a chair, her feet on a needlepoint stool, her fine hands knotted together. She kept moaning, "I don't know who it was. I was sitting there after I asked the detective to go for some medicine for Amy."

The detective came in with a package, confused when he saw all of us standing about, the marks of the scarf still on Miss Lovelace's throat. The Inspector lit into him and he defended himself as best he could. "She asked me . . . everything was quiet . . . said the old lady was very sick. Drugstore wasn't open . . . I had to stop at the doc's office . . ."

Carol and George stepped in. They couldn't stay away from that house of horror. They looked very happy until they heard. Miss Lovelace overheard the news of Brundage and broke into tears. The girls did their best to console her, while the Inspector again took up a questioning of suspects. It seemed to me that I would go batty listening to it again and again. "Where were you? Why? When?" Men from the Division moved in—all over again. It was like a nightmare—an endless nightmare.

We were gathered round. This time around one who hadn't died, while upstairs experts moved around Brundage. It was uncomfortably hot in the room . . . Oglesbie hurt my ears screaming at Lovelace, "Quit looking at me! I didn't do it! I haven't been in this room."

She spoke weakly, pathetically. "You came to the head of the stairs."

"Oh, my God!" He was tearing at his hair, hysterical now, "But I didn't come down! I saw you here and I went back."

She looked at him, not accusingly but sorrowfully, her eyes never leaving his face.

The Inspector turned to Phillips. "Can you add anything to tonight's mystery?"

"Me? Not a thing." He made a bolt for the door. "I want to get out of here! I'm going to ship out if a tin fish does get me . . . I can't stand it here!"

"You'll have to stay for a while. You might like to know that your friend, Kalski, is in jail. Everything he told you is lies—he was working for the German government. So, if and when we let you go, don't worry about the tin fish."

Phillips grunted, shuffled his feet, "I knew he was a phony."

"Were you in your room all night—and this morning, Phillips?"

"Hell, yes! This house scares the liver out of me. I wouldn't step my foot out . . ."

They were bringing down the body of poor Brundage. Phillips knew it when he stopped. I knew it when I looked at Lovelace, the convulsive shudder that sent her hands covering her eyes.

Down. Down. Down. Like a dull blow to the ears.

The Inspector spoke. "Bring the body in here!"

I looked at him. He was another Hitchcock—an uncanny sense of drama—diabolically making the most of each scene. Oglesbie startled the life out of me by grabbing my arm. "My God, Redfern, I can't stand it!" I pulled away but he moved closer. It was getting so warm that I felt like tearing my shirt off.

A corpse on a stretcher, the knees doubled up under the thin blanket, small brown hands twisted as they clutched at the last vestige of life. The Inspector's order, "Raise the head and wait outside!" Ah, yes, the head—grisly, horrible.

The dead staring open-eyed at the almost dead. Lovelace's hands dropped from her face. I expected her to shriek out at the sight, but she must have steeled herself—there was no sound. Her eyes wavered, settled on the corpse, then attached themselves to poor Oglesbie. I saw Lita put her hand up to her face—she was about to faint. I took her arm and drew her over to me. As I did so, I passed a radiator. "There's a fire in the furnace, Inspector!"

He jumped as though I had struck him. "Should have thought of that. Go down, Brandt—bring up what you can."

The telephone rang. The Inspector answered, leaving us standing helplessly, trying not to look at each other. He was more like himself when he came back—had command of the situation.

He moved the marble table forward. Laid the two sections of the ivory hand on it. He was doing all right with his props if he hadn't come prepared. A pity that he didn't have the grotesque shrunken head and dangling hand! And the decomposed body of Beauty! You can tell how I was feeling. I was sick unto death of the whole business. He knew who the murderer was; why didn't he strike and quit playing with us—like a large cat cornering mice?

When he smiled around at us, I knew he was ready to strike!

"Some person in this room told poor Mrs. Selton that she would be forever rid of her goitre if she would let them put this supposedly human hand down her throat without uttering a sound. She did and she was quickly strangled to death."

There was no sound or answer to this information. Lovelace stared with frightened eyes at Oglesbie.

Then he rolled out two sparkling blue earrings. I felt the shudder that went through Lita. But it was Carol who stole the limelight. "Those are Lita's!" Before I could strike her dead with my look, she went on breathlessly, "She lent them to me shortly after I came here. I—I thought I lost them. Where did you find them?"

"One was under the chair of death. The other was down her bodice."

I felt the carpet moving under me. What a fool I had been! Everybody was watching Carol, including Miss Lovelace. Carol looked sicker than I felt. "I don't know how they got there."

Brandt came up then with the fragments he had saved from the fire. "Couldn't get much. Maybe the lab can do something with them." I went close to the table where the Inspector placed them. Bits of newspaper, of a letter, charred cloth. Carol exclaimed, "That's green. Grandma had a smock." She looked up at me quickly. "Is that part of my letters?"

I shrugged, but the Inspector answered, "Undoubtedly your grandmother's smock. Somebody has been impersonating her, so they could have the house at night and prepare for more murder, if necessary. This last affair was meant to finish things—so the smock was burned, the scarves saved for the last strangling jobs."

He spoke harshly. "What are the letters?"

Carol answered, "Letters that my mother wrote to my grandmother. Mr. Redfern took them and I never saw them again."

He looked at me. "What did you do with them?"

"I put them in the highboy drawer. The 'ghost' that prowled around at night took them—before I put the padlock on."

"I see. That is your theory." His blandness irritated me. The room was hot. A furnace fire—larger than necessary to burn the bits of evidence. Somebody had been frightened and must have tossed on kindling. The sun was rising higher, adding its heat to the overheated room. Poor Brundage wasn't a pretty object in life—in death she was . . . I looked at Lovelace, frail, pitiful. How did she stand it? What was she thinking of? The last of the old gals who had been almost inseparable through most of their lives.

I saw her slump down in her chair. "Inspector! Miss Lovelace!"

He looked toward her, "Get her some water." I did better than that—I put a jigger of whiskey in it. When I got back the Inspector was holding a pair of white gloves. I stopped short. He told me they hadn't come from the laboratory yet. These had dirt clinging to them. They had been worn. The fingers cupped significantly as though reaching white hands . . . Lovelace sighed. I reached down, holding the glass to her lips. He was up to his old tricks—the gloves a substitute pair he had been waiting to spring on us as soon as he got the assurance from the laboratory.

Lovelace was sucking up the liquid, not at all genteelly. She had certainly been through a lot. She must be on the verge of collapse.

He put the gloves on the table reaching toward each other, the width of a throat between them. Then he took a letter out of his pocket. It was dirty, had been ground underfoot. I knew it was the one from Kalski's. It had fallen under our bodies. My body cringed at the memory of that struggle. The Inspector's suave voice, "This letter was written to bring a man here on the night of the murder. This man was to be a suspect in case the other suspects proved their innocence. Because Mrs. Selton's death was carefully planned—the minute she could no longer be controlled. She had had trouble with this man and, true to her nature, she ordered him out of the house. It was his voice that was heard quarreling with Mrs. Selton. You see, Mrs. Selton did not write the letter—she did not know he was coming."

He had his audience, every last one of them. I could hear Oglesbie's breathing—too quick and shallow to do him any good. I put the glass down and went over to comfort Lita with what was left of my manly strength.

After giving that much to his parched audience, the Inspector picked up a white glove, careful not to disturb the dirt that clung to it. He asked casually, "Has anyone missed a pair of white gloves?"

I felt Lita's body stiffen, her breath catch. The soft throaty sound of her voice tore at my heart. "I missed a pair after the murder."

"What size were they, Mrs. Redfern?"

"Size six."

He nodded as though he already knew. I was watching him, my fists clenched. If he played on her emotions, I knew that I would knock him down. But he turned politely to Carol. She answered his look, "I didn't miss any . . . I didn't have any, then." He studied her hands, finally passing on to George, to Phillips.

His smiling gaze stopped at Oglesbie. "You have a small hand, Doctor." As though they shared some intimate secret, he beamed at Lovelace, "What size would you say he wore, Miss Lovelace?"

Her body straightened and her eyes snapped. "I would say a seven and a half!"

The answer gave the Inspector complete satisfaction. He spoke softly. "I think you can wear this glove, Doctor. In fact, I think it would be a perfect fit."

Oglesbie was having the fit as the Inspector held the white glove toward the doctor. Especially when the Inspector added for good measure, "You wouldn't look conspicuous in a smock and scarf—at night." The doctor's face went slack, his eyes dull, and the soft hands wiped themselves over and over on the crushed handkerchief.

Highly amused, the Inspector turned briskly to Lovelace. "You try it on first, Miss Lovelace, for size."

Obediently she held her hand out. He pushed the glove down over the up-stretched fingers. Her eyes dilated as she held the white-gloved hand out, fingers spread. Not a sound, even of breathing.

Then a high scream that sent sound bursting against the staunch walls. She was clawing at the glove, tearing it, picking at it like a dying person, her face a twisted mask of death. The hideous din and violent contortions of the calm and genteel Lovelace made gaping statues out of all of us.

The Inspector leaned over, snapped the bracelets on her. "We will have to put you in a strait-jacket. You wouldn't want to be carried out of here screaming and clawing."

She looked at him, her face distorted with hate, but suddenly quiet, as he continued, "You strangled Mrs. Selton to keep her from changing her will!" He had plenty of time to bow whimsically at me. "Mr. Redfern would say—he is evidently a student of psychology—that you murdered her because you could no longer control her. It is his theory—" how the devil did he know my theory?— "that you meant to marry Thomas Selton. When fate decided otherwise, you made of yourself a serpent in their Garden of Eden. You drove them from each other and from happiness."

His mind was as quick as lightning, given the proper radio-activity. He held my admiration. "These letters that you burned were evidently the ones that you intercepted between the mother and daughter. You left the poor old mother grieving her life through, thinking that her daughter had never written."

Carol gasped. Miss Lovelace never took her eyes from the Inspector's face. "You, yourself, told me that the Redferns had forced Carol to go into that attic that first night to search for and destroy the will, so that the property would go to her and they would share. You would understand that. What you didn't tell me was that the trunk from which the letters were taken was undoubtedly yours. I realized that quite recently because the trunk was locked when I investigated later. The testimony I had from Phillips gave me no clue."

Lovelace's face didn't change as the twisted features

and disdainful eyes looked into his. Lita sagged against me. "Oh, Paul," she whispered, "it was she who tried to kill us!"

I pressed her arm, fascinated as the others were with the Inspector's recital, although I had been two jumps ahead of him. I looked over at Brundage, expecting her to interrupt, to challenge the Inspector. Those terrible eyes! Anguish and horror beyond belief or understanding! What had been her thoughts as she cried out against the tightening of that brilliant scarf? She knew now!

The Inspector's voice, harsher, hitting at Lovelace, "You strangled the cat because he was the only living thing that had seen you commit murder. He couldn't disclose the information but he showed his hatred of you. All the evidence, as you had foreseen, pointed to somebody else." Lita shivered in my arms.

"This letter—" He held up the soiled envelope, and I knew then that the paper inside was a substitute—the original was at the analyst, from whom he had received the information. "This letter was written by you to bring Kalski here on the night of the murder. At a casual glance, it was Mrs. Selton's writing." I remembered some of the contradictory notes that had made us question Mrs. Selton's sanity—and the last note that there would be no soiree! But I wanted to listen to Inspector Green. "You were late for tea that afternoon, as Miss Brundage would repeat if she were able to! It took time to get over to Scollay and watch the note being delivered."

She spoke now, her eyes as bright as a cornered rat's. "You can't prove it—you can't! There's nothing—no fingerprint!"

His triumphant gaze went to the glove on her hand, still held there by the handcuff. "You have the proof right there!" I knew it wasn't the right glove, but she didn't. "That glove fits nobody's hand but yours. It is a size seven. It is a shame that your harp-playing has developed your hands—for murder." He condescended to smile on Oglesbie. "In case you don't know—a seven and a half woman's glove is the smallest size you could wear. And one needs comfort when one sets out to murder."

There was panic in her eyes now. "That does not prove . . ."

He thundered, "It proves you broke the ivory hand . . . there are pieces of ivory clinging to that glove!"

She shrank down in her chair.

His words battered against her. "You strangled this woman here . . . the oldest friend you had in the world! You are inhuman, a monster of cruelty!"

She sneered from her ebbing superiority complex. "She said she would take care of me . . . of Evelyn Lovelace!"

"That was where she made her mistake. You had used her since girlhood, just as you used the Seltons." As though getting himself on safer ground, out of the theoretical, he added, "Your real reason was money. You had none. She had. Your devious mind thought up a way whereby you could get that money. Somebody else would burn . . . maybe two somebodies!"

Lita and I instinctively moved closer. She raised an adoring face, love-infused. Like a sailor on a park bench I forgot the others. My lips went down to rest on hers. We were together, united in our love. If I hadn't gone to Kalski's to get the letter! If she hadn't loved me enough to leave the apartment in search of me! We would have been on hand to sink deeper . . .

It didn't matter that Lovelace was screeching like a she-wolf. That Brundage was going out without sound. That Phillips was yelling, "Christ! Christ in the mountains! Stop that goddam yelling!" That they were taking the ladies out. That Oglesbie was pulling at my sleeve, begging me, "Redfern, do you think I could get a job in Washington?" That Carol was saying, "Paul! You and Lita can live here. It's quite unnecessary for you to move." I was laughing deep down inside of me. Oglesbie in Washington—why not? But Lita and I in Brattle? No! We'd move to the Back Bay across the Charles. Nice new places there, not more than seventy years old. Or on Beacon Hill . . . Move in with the immigrants, now that most of the oldsters were dried up. Nice, roomy, barn-like places less than three hundred years old . . .

A smart crack on the elbow brought me back to the drawing-room and the bland face of the Inspector. "The Grand Jury hasn't returned an indictment yet, Redfern. You are still obliged to answer questions. When did *you* first learn that Miss Lovelace was the murderess?"

I grinned, "When I stood on the stairs during the reading of the will. I could see only the top of Lovelace's head. I remembered that she had screamed before she left the stairs. She couldn't have known that Mrs. Selton was dead unless she went over almost in front of her."

I became expansive, a minor inspector. "Of course, I was suspicious long before that. She was the only one of us who wrote 'The Stroke of Death' without nervousness, because she was the only one who knew that Mrs. Selton had written it herself. I even kept one of the notes we got —the last one—it didn't look like Mrs. Selton's handwriting. I—I—"

His cynical smile was making me stutter. He moved away. The others too. Lita and I were alone. The love light hadn't left her eyes. "You're wonderful, Paul."

I bowed. It's nice to be married. "Madame, will you do me the honor of going to bed with me? I'm tired . . ."

A melodious ripple of throaty laughter. She was on to me too! She didn't believe I was tired.

THE END